MARMADUKE™

THE JUNIOR NOVEL

TWENTIETH CENTURY FOX AND REGENCY ENTERPRISES PRESENT A DAVIS ENTERTAINMENT COMPANY PRODUCTION A TOM DEY FILM "MARMADUKE" OWEN WILSON AS THE VOICE OF "MARMADUKE" LEE PACE JUDY GREER AND WILLIAM H. MACY STEVE COOGAN SAM ELLIOTT STACY FERGUSON GEORGE LOPEZ CHRISTOPHER MINTZ-PLASSE EMMA STONE KIEFER SUTHERLAND MARLON WAYANS MUSIC SUPERVISOR DAVE JORDAN & JOJO VILLANUEVA MUSIC BY CHRISTOPHER LENNERTZ COSTUME DESIGNER KAREN MATTHEWS FILM EDITOR DON ZIMMERMAN, A.C.E. DIRECTOR OF PHOTOGRAPHY GREG GARDNER EXECUTIVE PRODUCERS ARNON MILCHAN TARIQ JALIL JEFFREY STOTT BASED UPON THE COMIC CREATED BY BRAD ANDERSON AND PHIL LEEMING WRITTEN BY TIM RASMUSSEN & VINCE DI MEGLIO PRODUCED BY JOHN DAVIS DIRECTED BY TOM DEY

www.themarmadukemovie.com

HarperFestival is an imprint of HarperCollins Publishers.

Library of Congress catalog card number: 2009943953
ISBN 978-0-06-199506-4

Typography by Rick Farley
10 11 12 13 14 LP/CW 10 9 8 7 6 5 4 3 2 1
❖
First Edition

MARMADUKE™

THE JUNIOR NOVEL

Based upon the comic created by
BRAD ANDERSON and **PHIL LEEMING**
Written by
TIM RASMUSSEN & **VINCE DI MEGLIO**
Adapted by
J. E. BRIGHT

HARPER FESTIVAL
An Imprint of HarperCollinsPublishers

CHAPTER 1

Marmaduke the Great Dane yawned as he wandered into the kitchen, where his family was already eating breakfast. In the corner, Carlos, a fluffy Russian blue cat, was eating kibble out of his food bowl.

Marmaduke's bowl was next to Carlos's, and it was full of leftovers. *Waffles,* he thought in satisfaction. *Gotta love Debbie!*

"'Sup," Carlos greeted Marmaduke.

"Hey, man," Marmaduke replied. He thought his stepbrother, Carlos, was pretty cool for a cat. Which was good, since Carlos was basically his only friend.

"You ready for a bombshell?" Carlos asked. "Phil just told everybody he got a new job. We're

1

moving to California."

"Shut up." Marmaduke gasped.

Carlos shook his head. "No lie," he replied. "I was so shocked, I hacked that up." He raised his chin toward a large, wet ball of fur on the tile floor.

Marmaduke wrinkled up his nose. "That's not your hair."

Carlos nodded, closing his eyes. "Long night," he said wearily.

After finishing off his waffles, Marmaduke headed over to the human table, where Phil and Debbie were still explaining the move to the family. Three-year-old Sarah didn't really understand. Brian was engrossed in his handheld video game, while Barbara was staring sullenly down at her plate.

"But all my friends are here," Barbara complained.

Phil patted her on the hand. "I hear you, honey, but you'll make new friends," he said. "And I'll be making enough money that you can text all you want." He reached over and raised the visor of Brian's baseball cap. "Bri?"

"I dunno," Brian mumbled. "Sounds okay, I guess."

"What do you care?" Barbara snapped at her brother. "You live in your head anyway. This is so unfair!"

Marmaduke had to agree with Barbara. He had more bones buried in the backyard than he could count. It would take weeks to find them all! He laid his head on Barbara's leg, and she scratched him behind the ears.

"I know it's hard, guys," Phil continued, "but we're outgrowing this place. The O.C. has beaches and sunshine. We'll have a big new house with a pool and a company car. It's the chance to have everything we've ever wanted."

Pets are the last to find out anything, Marmaduke thought. *And I don't even know where the O.C.'s at!*

The O.C. turned out to stand for Orange County, which was a wealthy area of California south of Los Angeles, famous for its beautiful weather and Pacific Ocean beaches. The moving day came quickly, and before Marmaduke realized what was happening, a moving van was parked outside the house. The movers rapidly filled the van up with everything the Winslows were taking with them.

Marmaduke watched from his giant travel crate as Phil and Brian stood in the driveway saying good-bye to the neighbors. Debbie watched with concern as her daughter sobbed in a huddle of her friends, all thirteen-year-old girls. As a mover passed by Barbara, carrying a pink floor lamp, Barbara grabbed it, and she and the mover got into a tug of war.

Carlos was sitting in a small travel crate atop Marmaduke's humongous one. "This is a horrible mistake!" the cat screeched. "I requested executive class!"

Phil appeared in front of the grilles of their crates. He held up a paper bag and smiled. "Hey, guys, look what I got," he told his pets. "A special snack for the plane ride." Phil pulled meatballs out of the bag and opened the crates so he could give them to the animals.

Marmaduke sniffed his meatball suspiciously. "Am I missing something?"

"They're Debbie's special meatballs, man," Carlos said. "Don't question it."

The dog and cat wolfed down the meatballs.

Marmaduke raised an eyebrow when he saw Phil smiling knowingly, but the tastiness of the meatball erased all his worries. *This is great,* he thought. *I take back everything I ever said about Phil!*

The next hours passed in a blur. Marmaduke sort of remembered his crate being in a large, dark chamber, with the whooshing roar of a huge engine echoing all around. He had a fuzzy memory of Carlos talking to him in the plane.

"Have you ever looked at your paws?" Carlos asked groggily. "I mean really looked at them?"

"I think Phil put something in those meatballs," Marmaduke mumbled.

Both the cat and dog struggled to stay upright inside their crates.

"Stay awake, *amigo*!" Carlos insisted. "Fight it!"

But Marmaduke was too dizzy. "I followed you into many adventures," he told his friend, his eyes rolling up in his head, "but into the Great Unknown Mystery, I go first, Carlos!"

Then Marmaduke fell over onto his side inside the crate, with a smile on his lips.

While Marmaduke was in his stupor, he dreamed about riding around in a red convertible, his ears flapping in the warm breeze. Overhead he could see the tops of palm trees arching over the sides of the highway. The sky was cloudless, and sunshine twinkled on the clean sidewalks, which were populated by beautiful, pampered white poodles wearing sunglasses.

"Wake up, guys," Debbie said. "Welcome to your new house."

Marmaduke blinked as Phil opened the crates. He peered out and saw that he was beside tall stacks of moving boxes in a new living room. The house was gorgeous, with wide rooms, dark hardwood floors, and tall arched windows. It was dark outside, but Marmaduke could tell that during the day the room would be bright and sunny.

It wasn't easy climbing out of the crate—the room seemed to be spinning slightly, and Marmaduke's family looked blurry. He stood up in the new living room. "I'm up!" he barked.

Then he stumbled. "I'm down!" Marmaduke crashed into a pile of boxes, knocking them over with a loud thump.

"Give me twelve more of those meatballs right now!" Carlos insisted.

That was all Marmaduke remembered until

the morning, when the alarm clock woke him up. He'd been sleeping between Phil and Debbie on the bed in their new bedroom. Carlos was curled up in a cat bed on the floor.

Marmaduke bolted out of bed, knocking Phil over the side. "Good morning, Orange County!" Marmaduke barked, and he raced into the hall.

Phil pushed himself up off the floorboards. "Same dog," he grumbled, "different floor."

While the rest of his family was waking up, Marmaduke rushed around the house, inspecting all the different rooms and corners, zooming around packing boxes, sniffing everything he could reach. "New city!" he barked. "New house! New smells!"

Downstairs in the spacious, modern kitchen, Marmaduke discovered a doggie door built just his size. He pushed himself outside easily and found he was in a wide, green backyard with a pool just beyond it.

Marmaduke took a moment to breathe in the fresh air and admire his new home. "This is by far the nicest bathroom I've ever had!" he cheered.

After breakfast, Phil put a new collar on

Marmaduke while Debbie put a new pink tie on Phil.

A new life means new accessories, Marmaduke thought. *Mmm, that new collar smell!*

"Is it weird that your boss wants to meet you at the dog park?" Debbie asked Phil as she continued tying his tie. "Chin up."

Phil raised his head so Debbie could reach the tie knot more easily.

Marmaduke rushed over to the front door. "Come on, Phil!" he barked. "Let's go!"

"That's how they roll in Cali," Phil replied to Debbie. "He's a bit eccentric maybe, but that's why he's so successful."

"That's how they roll in Cali." She patted the completed tie knot. "Don't worry about me. I'll be here unpacking a thousand boxes."

Phil gave her a soft kiss. "I promise I'll be home early to help."

As Phil opened the front door, Debbie peered around his shoulder and looked surprised by what she saw in the driveway. "That's the company car?"

The car was a brand-new, small, two-door; very cute, but perhaps not the best choice for a family with a giant Great Dane for a pet. Phil and Marmaduke climbed in, and the dog had to stick his head out of the sunroof to sit comfortably. As they zoomed along the roads toward the park, other drivers gawked at Marmaduke's big head popping out of the top of the tiny car, his ears flapping in the breeze.

At the large, beautifully landscaped park, Phil pulled the car into the parking lot. Marmaduke could hardly sit still as Phil hooked a leash onto his collar.

"Listen, buddy," Phil said, "things work differently out here, okay? We've got to impress my boss. I need you to be good—very good. Basically, the opposite of you."

Marmaduke wagged his tail, thinking that Phil had nothing to worry about. He had a chance to completely reinvent himself and finally make friends. *I've got a new leash on life,* Marmaduke thought. *Pun intended.*

Phil and Marmaduke made their way to the park entrance, where they paused, taking in the green splendor. Tall trees rustled in the breeze near gorgeous beds of multicolored flowers. Ducks and swans glided across a large blue pond in the middle of the park. Kids played Frisbee close to a few picnic tables. Best of all was the wide meadow where dozens of dogs romped with their owners.

Both Marmaduke and Phil took deep breaths. "New life, here I come!" they said together.

As they walked along the park's paths, Marmaduke noticed that certain groups of dogs were hanging out, separate from other types of dogs. They passed by a cluster of little female lapdogs. "So I said," a sassy Pomeranian told a toy poodle, "if you want to be with me, you'd better change that tone of bark."

"Good for you, girl," the poodle replied.

Shocked at the size of Marmaduke, the Pomeranian and the poodle both stopped talking as he passed by.

Marmaduke looked away nervously, spotting two taller Airedales chatting nearby. One of the Airedales looked nauseous as he munched grass. "Why did I drink all of that toilet water?" the Airedale asked. "My head's killing me."

"Eat more grass," the second Airedale suggested. "You'll feel better."

But the advice was forgotten as the Airedales

saw Marmaduke. They did a double take. "Holy cow," the first Airedale muttered.

Marmaduke started feeling even more nervous as all the dogs in the park stopped what they were doing to stare at him. *Think small,* he told himself. *Play it cool!* He nodded at a bulldog wearing a knitted varsity vest. "Cool sweater," Marmaduke told him.

Despite Marmaduke's friendliness, the other dogs all whispered to one another as he continued down the path with Phil.

"Welcome to Jurassic Dog Park," a bichon frise mumbled to a dachshund.

A teacup poodle trembled at the sight of the Great Dane. "Please let him be an herbivore!" she whispered.

As Marmaduke and Phil reached the middle of the dog meadow, where a gazebo gave owners some shade and a watering station relieved thirsty dogs, a deep voice rang out from a man sitting on a wooden bench along the path.

"Winslow!" the man called. "Over here!"

CHAPTER 2

Phil yanked Marmaduke's leash sharply, leading him over to Phil's new boss, Don Twombly. Don was in his early fifties, with grayish-blond hair and a big mustache. He seemed very sure of himself. Don and Phil shook hands.

"Mr. Twombly," Phil said, "great to see you again."

"Morning," Don replied. Then he noticed Phil's tie. "Pink. Interesting choice."

Phil ran his hand down the tie. "Thanks," he said. "It's more like fuchsia."

Don smirked. "Are you saying I don't know pink from fuchsia?"

"No," Phil said quickly. "Uh . . . you know—"

"Relax," Don interrupted. "I'm just messing

with you." He clapped Phil on the shoulder. "But it is pink."

Marmaduke let out a short, friendly bark, and Don kneeled beside him. "Who do we have here?" he asked.

"That's Marmaduke," Phil answered.

"Marmaduke," Don repeated, ruffling the fur on the dog's head. "You're a really handsome Great Dane, you know that?"

Marmaduke wagged his tail. *I'm starting to like this guy,* he thought.

Don peered up at Phil. "You've got yourself a beautiful best friend here."

"Thank you," Phil replied. "Marmaduke and I are like two peas in a pod."

Then Don leaned forward to give Marmaduke a deep sniff. "Interesting," he said. "I'm picking up something else here, too. He's definitely not a purebred. I'm sensing a little English mastiff, about an eighth, I'm guessing." He raised Marmaduke's lips and checked out his teeth.

"Hey, watch it, man," Marmaduke muttered.

Phil shrugged. "Your guess is as good as mine."

Don glanced up sharply. "Do you even know your own best friend, Phil?"

"Sure," Phil replied. He flapped his hands uneasily. "You know . . ."

Standing up, Don began circling around Phil, and Phil had to pivot to maintain eye contact. "I love dogs," Don said. "I can tell a lot about a man by the way he treats his dog. I think if people took their cues from canines, we'd be better off as a species. It's why I like working out here. I can measure firsthand who I'm dealing with." Don took a deep breath. "Plus there's fresh air for out-of-the-box thinking, and most importantly, I get to spend more quality time with my little girl, Jezebel."

Don pointed across the meadow. Phil and Marmaduke turned to see an elegant collie lapping water from a bowl near the gazebo.

Hello, gorgeous! Marmaduke thought.

With a smile, Don put his hands on his hips. "What a princess, huh?"

"Yes, sir," Phil replied. "Very beautiful."

Don played with a half-heart-shaped pendant hanging on a silver chain around his neck. Jezebel wore a matching pendant on her collar.

"She's very particular about who she spends time with," Don said, looking at Marmaduke. "So don't let your big boy there get any wild ideas, huh?"

"Who you calling 'big boy'?" Marmaduke barked.

With a laugh, Don smacked Phil on the arm, and Phil smiled nervously. "Now," Don ordered, "take off your shoes and let's walk."

Phil looked down. Don was already barefoot. "You don't wear shoes out here?"

"Do dogs wear shoes?" Don shot back.

Phil rubbed his chin. "Is that a trick question?"

"Come on," Don said. "Channel your inner canine. Feel the earth between your toes!"

"It's not the earth I'm worried about," Phil mumbled. But he pulled off his shoes and socks and tiptoed after Don, who was striding across the meadow.

Phil had disconnected Marmaduke from his leash so he could play. While Phil was busy with Don, Marmaduke discovered that two small mutts stood close behind him, sniffing his butt.

"Upper Darby, Pennsylvania?" a geeky part-dachshund wondered, trying to guess where Marmaduke was from by his smell. "Southern Ohio Valley?"

A scrawny Chinese crested mix took a sniff, too. He had a hairless torso, but a shock of white head hair that looked like a fright wig. "Long Beach?" the strange-looking dog guessed. "Fresno?"

"Whoa!" Marmaduke cried, whirling around. "Easy, fellas!"

A female mutt who looked like she was mostly Queensland heeler sauntered over. Queensland heelers were also known as Australian cattle dogs, and they were bred for the hard work of rounding up livestock. She was medium-sized, with patchy gray-and-brown fur on her body and a black mask on her face. Swaggering like a tomboy, the female took a sniff, too. "I'm going to say Kansas," she decided.

"Wow," Marmaduke said, impressed. "Kansas. How did you know?"

"It's a gift," the female mutt replied. "What's your handle, newbie?"

"Marmaduke," Marmaduke answered.

"Yikes," she said, grimacing. "Immediately

moving on, meet the gang." She nodded at the wiry part-dachshund. "The egghead here is Raisin."

"Marmaduke," Raisin repeated, with a nerdy snort. "A unique synthesis of *marma*, the scientific name for the jumping spider family . . . and the Duke of Marlborough, the seventeenth-century English statesman. Am I right?"

Marmaduke blinked at Raisin. Then he had a strong memory of himself as a puppy on Christmas morning, when he'd first arrived at the Winslows' house in Kansas. Young Barbara was sitting on one side of him, and little Brian sat on the other side.

"Marmalade!" Barbara had insisted.

"Duke!" Brian had argued.

"Marmalade!"

"Duke!"

Shaking his head to clear the memory of how he got his mixed-up name, Marmaduke nodded seriously at Raisin. "Yep, you nailed it."

"I knew it," Raisin replied with another snort. "I rarely miss."

"Except when girls are involved," the tomboyish female added. Then she raised her muzzle toward the weird, trembling Chinese crested mix. "Mr. Self-Confidence over here is named Giuseppe."

"Before you ask," Giuseppe said quickly, "no, I didn't just drink a pot of coffee, and no, I'm not cold. I just get a little anxious sometimes. This is California, land of the puma." The shaking dog lowered his voice to a whisper. "They come out of nowhere."

The female Queensland heeler mix thumped her tail. "He's half Chinese crested, half gremlin," she said. "Both halves are nervous wrecks. I'm Mazie, by the way."

Marmaduke smiled. "The meddling ringleader who talks a good game, right?" Mazie dipped her muzzle. "Touché," she said, surprised at his insight.

"Good to meet you guys," Marmaduke told them. "You come here a lot?"

Mazie barked out a laugh. "It's the dog park, man," she said. "It's like high school for dogs." She peered around the meadow. "Which means there're a few packs to know about."

Marmaduke peered around for Phil. He seemed busy talking to Don, so Marmaduke followed along as Mazie led their little gang through the meadow.

"First, you got your jocks," Mazie instructed. She pointed her muzzle toward a group of buff dogs jumping around playing Frisbee. Female cocker spaniels with bows in their hair sat nearby, swooning and giggling over the muscular jocks.

"The only muscle the jocks don't use is their brain," Mazie explained. "They mostly date cocker spaniels . . . who actually have no brains."

One jock missed catching a Frisbee, and the plastic disk bonked a cocker spaniel on her head. She smiled. "Frisbee!" she squealed.

Mazie kept walking and gestured over to where two dogs were sitting attentively in front of their trainer. "Then you got your drama geeks," Mazie said.

The trainer cocked his finger like he was shooting a gun at the dogs. Both dogs fell over dramatically, playing dead.

"The short one just landed a national dog food commercial," Raisin said. "I hear he's getting a lifetime supply."

"He's got a great agent," added Giuseppe.

With a deep breath, Marmaduke sat down

on the grass. "Wow, big choices," he said. "I'm not sure which pack to hang with."

Mazie nodded. "Well, if you think you've got game, you can roll with our crew."

"Yeah?" Marmaduke asked, his ears perking up. "Who's your crew?"

"Mutts!" two miniature Doberman pinschers answered as they zoomed by. Laughing, the two min pins scurried over to where a big, muscular, black-and-brown Beauceron was surrounded by fancy-looking dogs in the shade of a stand of palm trees.

"Who are those guys?" Marmaduke asked.

"The pedigrees," Raisin replied with a snort. "Trouble."

Giuseppe shuddered. "They're rich and spoiled and think their meadow muffins don't stink."

Mazie glared at the miniature Doberman pinschers. "The land shrimps are Thunder and Lightning," she explained. "Dog Vader over there is the man himself, Bosco. He's the alpha male who runs the park, the toughest dog around." Mazie turned to look seriously into Marmaduke's eyes. "Bosco's girlfriend is Jezebel and he's super jealous, so stay away from her or he'll turn you into—"

"Dog food?" a deep voice finished for her.

Marmaduke raised his head to see that Bosco, Thunder, and Lightning had come close enough to overhear. Giuseppe quickly ducked behind Raisin to hide.

"Speak of the devil," Mazie growled.

"Hello, losers," Bosco sneered, sauntering closer. "Who's the new mutt?"

"Marmaduke," Marmaduke replied, trying to sound friendly.

"It speaks," snarled Bosco. He strode directly toward Marmaduke, who instinctively backed up a step and sat down. Bosco got right up into Marmaduke's face and smirked at him. Marmaduke gulped, even though he was the bigger dog.

"It's your first day, donkey boy," Bosco growled, "so let me tell you how it is. You cross into pedigree territory, you're dead. You put your nose in the wrong place, you're dead. You look at my girlfriend, you're—"

"Dead!" Lightning piped up.

Bosco glared at Lightning, but the min pin just shrugged.

"I think you get the point," Bosco told

Marmaduke. "Welcome to the O.C., mutt."

Thunder stepped forward, oddly menacing for a dog so small. "Steer clear, horsey."

"See you at the party tonight," Lightning said. "Not." He jumped forward at Marmaduke, and he laughed when the big dog flinched. All the pedigreed dogs joined in with Lightning's laughter, sauntering back toward their area under the palms.

Marmaduke sighed. "That royally sucked."

"Entitlement is so charming," replied Mazie.

Raisin snorted. "Don't listen to that guy," he said, baring his teeth toward Bosco.

"Maybe listen to the part about staying away from his girlfriend," Giuseppe suggested, "or he'll kill you. But other than that, yeah, ignore him."

"What party was Lightning talking about?" Marmaduke asked.

Mazie shook her head, jingling the tags on her collar. "Nothing," she said. "Just a bunch of snobs scratching themselves under the yacht club pier. We're having our own party at my place tonight. It's going to be a classic O.C. rager." She peered up at Marmaduke. "You should come."

"Yeah?" Marmaduke replied. "That sounds

really cool."

"You'll love it," Mazie said. She started to lope away, followed by Raisin and Giuseppe. "See you tonight!"

Marmaduke watched them head over to their owners on the other side of the meadow. He looked around for Phil and spotted him still talking to Don while walking gingerly through a patch of tall grass.

Not too bad, Marmaduke thought. *True, I almost got my tail handed to me in the first ten minutes here, but I've also got a new crew and a killer O.C. rager to go to. Things are looking pretty—*

A bee landed on Marmaduke's snout. His eyes crossed as he stared at it in alarm.

"Bee!" he screamed.

Marmaduke panicked, barking and bucking as he tried to shake off the bee. He raced toward Phil, with the pedigreed dogs laughing behind him at his freak-out.

"Bark Organics is the healthiest dog food around," Don was saying to Phil. "We have an enormous obligation to get Bark onto the shelves of every pet store in this country. Which is why I brought you out here from Kansas, Dorothy—to create a dynamic new ad campaign that appeals to the everyman. I'm just hoping you work out better than the last six directors."

"You fired six guys before me?" Phil asked.

"Of course not," Don replied. "What do you think I am? Three quit under the pressure."

Phil set his jaw firmly. "I won't let you down, sir," he said.

Then Marmaduke barreled through them, knocking Don onto the grass.

"Was that your dog?" Don demanded.

"Uh," Phil said. "I didn't get a good look."

As Phil was helping Don back onto his feet, Marmaduke zoomed back from the other direction, smashing Don in the crotch. Don collapsed in a moaning heap.

"Oh, that dog," said Phil.

Marmaduke blazed past the pedigrees under their palms.

"What a gargantuan spaz," sneered Bosco.

"I think he's interesting," said Jezebel.

Bosco glared at her. "Not really," he growled.

But Jezebel stared at Marmaduke galloping across the meadow and smiled.

CHAPTER 3

Later that night, Marmaduke followed Phil through the downstairs rooms of the house as Phil turned off the lights while chatting on his cell phone.

"Right," Phil told Don on the phone. "Regional market share first, then we'll make a move for the shelves. Sounds great. Talk to you tomorrow."

Bedtime, Philly, Marmaduke thought. *This dog has a rager to sneak out to!*

Phil headed up to his bedroom, where he found his wife eating leftover pizza while sitting at a small table near the windows. He kissed Debbie, and she handed him a slice of cold pizza. Phil sat down beside her and raised the pizza to his mouth.

All right! Marmaduke thought. *Pizza!* He jumped in between Phil and Debbie and gobbled the pizza before it reached Phil's lips.

Phil sighed. "That was my dinner," he complained, and Debbie gave him her half-eaten crust. "Listen," he said to her, "what do you think about hiring a dog trainer?"

"Trainer?" gasped Marmaduke.

Carlos laughed from where he was curled up nearby on a cushy chair. "Busted," the cat gloated.

"I don't know," Debbie replied. "We didn't have a trainer back in Kansas."

Marmaduke nudged Phil with his nose. "She makes a great point," he woofed.

"I didn't have to bring my dog to work in Kansas," Phil said, chewing on the pizza crust. "And he knocked over my boss today. Twice."

Debbie laughed. "I hope he has good insurance!"

"It's not funny," Phil said. "Don's a total kook about dogs. He judges you on how you are with them, and I've got enough to worry about without the bullet train here making me look bad." He ruffled the fur on Marmaduke's head.

Debbie ran her hand along Marmaduke's back. "What if *you* tried training him?" she asked. "Maybe he'd respond to that."

I'm totally sure I would, Marmaduke agreed.

Phil shook his head. "Did the Japanese train Godzilla not to invade Tokyo? No, they called in the National Guard." He paused a moment as Debbie stared blankly at him, but then he forged ahead. "I'm telling you, our dog is off the rails and we need professional help."

"I just never thought of us as a dog trainer family," Debbie argued.

Marmaduke put his head in her lap. "Hold your ground, Deb!" he whined.

"Trust me," Phil said. "We are now."

Debbie sighed. "Okay," she conceded, "if it's something you really think you need to do."

Marmaduke grunted. "And now I must turn my back on you forever," he told Debbie, raising his head off her lap and turning around.

"Things are going to change around here, mister," Phil said to Marmaduke.

"Come on," Debbie said, "you'll hurt his feelings."

"Trust me," Phil repeated, "he doesn't listen

to a thing I say."

Debbie crossed her arms over her chest. "He listens to me," she said softly.

Later that night, Marmaduke lay awake between Phil and Debbie on their bed until he was sure they both were fast asleep. As he waited, he could hear Carlos talking in his sleep in his cat bed.

"Beg for your life, hamster," Carlos muttered.

Marmaduke glanced around and began to wriggle his way out of the bed. Suddenly, Phil flipped over and threw his arm around Marmaduke, trapping him. Marmaduke tried to slide out from under Phil's arm, but Phil held him tight.

After a few minutes of wondering how to escape, Marmaduke flicked Phil's nose with his tail. Phil raised his arm to scratch his nose, and Marmaduke slithered free.

Sweet dreams, Philly, Marmaduke thought.

Just as Marmaduke was about to step off the end of the bed, the mattress squeaked, and Phil's eyes popped open. Marmaduke froze as he and Phil stared at each other.

Slowly, Phil's eyelids drooped shut again. When he was back to breathing regularly,

Marmaduke tiptoed out of the bedroom.

Marmaduke exited out his doggie door and hurried through backyards until he reached Mazie's house on the other side of the neighborhood. He heard dance music blaring through the garage door, so he trotted up and scratched on it.

After a moment, the garage door slowly retracted upward, and Marmaduke stepped inside.

The space inside the garage had been decorated with secondhand furniture—an old table, an older, soiled couch, an old-school TV, and a video game system, all atop a patchy rug. Near the door, Mazie was standing on a high box so she could reach the garage door controls. As soon as Marmaduke was fully inside, Mazie pressed a button with her paw, and the garage door slid slowly shut.

Raisin was sitting on the couch, watching Giuseppe play a dancing game on the rug in front of the TV.

This wasn't the rager Marmaduke was expecting—not even close!

"What up, dude!" Raisin called to Marmaduke. "Come watch Giuseppe rip it up!"

"Get a hip injury is more like it," Giuseppe

said, as he wriggled along with the game's music. "I'm genetically predisposed."

Marmaduke glanced around the garage, sniffing. "This is the O.C. rager?"

"I know," Mazie said, "it's out of control. If you're hungry or thirsty, the trash can's out back." She nodded her head toward a door that led to the house. "And the toilet's in there."

Marmaduke walked toward the couch. He was startled when he stepped on something that let out a loud *oink!* Looking down, he saw that he'd squashed a squeaky toy shaped like a cow.

Raisin and Giuseppe laughed. "Meet Mazie's cow," Raisin said. "The factory made a mistake. It's pretty ridiculous."

"She chews it when she gets nervous," Giuseppe added.

Marmaduke stepped on the cow again, and once again it oinked.

Mazie ducked her head in embarrassment. "They think Pig Cow is lame, but he's always been there for me when I need him."

"A cow that oinks," said Marmaduke. "I think it's cool."

Peering up at him, Mazie looked surprised,

but then she smiled.

"A new record!" Giuseppe cheered as his game ended. "Holla at your boy! Marmaduke, you're up."

Marmaduke shook his head. "It's cool," he said. "I'll just watch."

"Don't be a wiener dog," Raisin scolded, although he was partly dachshund himself. "Just dance along to the flashing arrows. A cocker spaniel could do it."

"Duke! Duke! Duke!" Raisin, Mazie, and Giuseppe all cheered.

"All right," Marmaduke said. "Twist my paw." He stepped onto the dance pad.

Mazie hit the start button, and music filled the garage as the game began.

Marmaduke danced along awkwardly.

"The boy's got mad coordination," Mazie said sarcastically.

"Bite me," Marmaduke replied, concentrating on dancing.

"Ease into it," Raisin suggested. "Feel the music."

"Let it wash over you like a flea bath," Giuseppe added.

As the game continued, Marmaduke gained some confidence and danced faster, hitting more of the pads the arrows indicated.

"He's feeling it," said Mazie.

"He's already beaten my record," Raisin said.

Giuseppe laughed. "Twenty seconds isn't hard to beat."

"I get leg cramps!" Raisin said defensively. "You know that."

Marmaduke barked happily. "Watch and learn, suckas!" he yelped, and he tried a fancy 360-degree spin move. His tail whacked into the console, knocking it to the floor with a loud crash.

The dogs all stared in silence at the broken game system.

Giuseppe groaned, covering his eyes with his paws. "My entire social life just went down the drain," he whimpered.

"I'm really sorry, guys," Marmaduke said, hanging his head.

"No sweat," Mazie replied. "I needed to get a new one anyway."

Raisin curled up on the couch and looked glum. "What are we going to do now?"

"What about checking out that pedigree party?" asked Marmaduke.

"Are you crazy?" Raisin demanded, his ears back flat against his head.

"We're mutts," Giuseppe said. "They hate us."

"Come on," Marmaduke wheedled, "it'll be fun. They're no different from us—we've got four legs, they've got four legs. I mean, have you guys ever been there before?"

"Well, no," Raisin admitted.

Marmaduke glanced at Mazie. "So?" he asked.

Mazie shrugged. "All right," she decided. "Some dogs just have to learn the hard way."

A little while later, the four mutts had left the neighborhood and were heading down a dark dirt path near a dry concrete aqueduct.

"How much farther?" Marmaduke asked.

"Relax," Mazie said. "We're almost there."

Giuseppe peered up at the cloudless sky nervously. "I smell rain."

"We're in the middle of a drought," said Raisin with a snort. "Look at the aqueduct. Water levels are the lowest in a decade."

"Just saying," Giuseppe replied nervously, "if

it does rain, the aqueduct could fill up, overflow, cause mud slides, sinkholes, and we'd all be swept away in a tidal wave, never to be seen again." He shuddered. "It's the perfect storm."

Mazie hopped over a broken branch on the path. "You're both hopeless."

Suddenly, far down the path, a wild-looking, muscular mastiff stepped into the light under a dim streetlamp. His eyes blazed frighteningly at the mutts.

The mutts halted on the path, hardly daring to breathe.

After a long, tense moment, the mastiff turned his head and walked off the path, disappearing into the dark underbrush.

Marmaduke let out a deep breath. "What was that?"

"Chupadogra," Mazie hissed. "He lives out by the railroad tracks."

Raisin snorted worriedly. "They say he was the ultimate alpha dog. Nobody crossed him. But then he went insane from rabies and ate his owner."

"He also sleeps on a giant pile of his victim's bones," Giuseppe added, trembling. "Can we go now before I become an appetizer?"

With Mazie leading the way, the mutts continued down the path.

But Marmaduke paused momentarily, staring at the spot where the mastiff had vanished into the bushes, before hurrying to catch up to his friends.

CHAPTER 4

The mutts finally arrived at a ritzy club on a raised pier on the edge of the ocean, beside a dark marina filled with the wobbling masts of sailboats and the shadowy shapes of yachts. Party music wafted out of the club, echoing over the moonlit water. Mazie led her friends under the pier, where pedigreed dogs of all breeds partied on the beach.

Marmaduke noticed several peds lapping up the liquid from a sewer run-off pipe, which seemed to make them tipsy. "Pretty crazy," he breathed.

By one of the pier supports, a sick-looking bulldog was being cheered on by two Dobermans as he gobbled hot dogs out of a big package.

"Twenty-six!" one Doberman announced.

"Don't hurl, dude!" the other Doberman insisted.

Giuseppe began shivering in indignation. "Cannibals!" he hissed.

"For the hundredth time," Raisin explained with a snort, "hot dogs aren't made from real dogs. They're made from rats."

Marmaduke's eyes gleamed as he stared at the party. It was a little wild and scary, but it looked like fun!

Mazie nudged him with her shoulder. "Seen enough?"

Marmaduke shook his head, and they walked closer to the center of the party. Directly under the pier, Marmaduke saw a group of dogs gathered in a circle, cheering. He could make out Thunder and Lightning chasing a terrified cat through the crowd, with Bosco egging them on.

"What are they doing?" Marmaduke asked, shocked.

"What peds do best," Mazie replied bitterly. "Humiliating the innocent!"

Marmaduke stepped to the side to avoid a shell in the sand, and he bumped into someone. He turned and found himself face-to-face with

Jezebel. She looked gorgeous, with her long, lustrous fur flowing in the ocean breeze.

"Sorry," Marmaduke muttered.

Jezebel shrugged, not quite smiling. "No problem."

Marmaduke started to walk to the left, but Jezebel was heading in the same direction. He stopped and turned right just as she did the same. Both dogs looked at each other and laughed awkwardly.

"This unfortunately happens to me all the time," Marmaduke admitted.

Mazie rolled her eyes. Then she noticed that Bosco was stomping his way across the sand, looking very irritated. "Great," Mazie said, "we're getting mad dogged. Let's bail!"

Before the mutts could leave, Bosco bounded over and blocked them. "Look what the cat dragged in," he growled. "It's the dog and pony show. The circus give you guys the day off?"

"We were just leaving, Bosco," Mazie said. "Back off."

Bosco smiled, revealing his sharp canine teeth. "But you just got here, tomboy."

Mazie and the other mutts shifted nervously

on the sand as more peds ambled over to watch the confrontation.

"Come on," Bosco continued, "join the party. I won't bite."

A mean laugh rumbled up from the pedigreed dogs around Bosco.

Marmaduke stepped forward, his legs wobbling.

Bosco glared at him. "With ears like that, you'd think you would've heard me say stay away from my girlfriend," he growled. "This is an exclusive pedigree party, mutt. Do you have any idea what that means?"

"Um," mumbled Marmaduke.

"Being a pedigree means you're exceptional," Bosco explained. "We're all bred for a purpose, and we have gifts you could never dream of having." He nodded his muzzle toward a stocky basset hound. "Stuart's an expert tracker." Bosco pointed out a thickly furred Alaskan malamute. "Shasta's a master sled dog." Last, he glanced over at a small, puffy Yorkie. "Ferdinand there is fluent in six languages, including Gopher."

Ferdinand let out a strange chirp that Marmaduke assumed gophers would understand.

"And I'm the reigning SoCal surf champ," Bosco bragged. "Are you good at anything? Huh?" He laughed loudly, and all the other peds joined in. Abruptly, Bosco whirled around to face Marmaduke. "Sit!" he ordered.

Marmaduke sat.

Bosco chuckled. "Oh, so you are good at something!"

Marmaduke hung his head in embarrassment as the peds cracked up again.

"I don't care how freakishly large you are," Bosco told Marmaduke, leaning in close to the bigger dog. "We both know on the inside you're just a scared little puppy dog. Now lie down."

After a second of hesitation, Marmaduke started to stand up.

"Did I say you could get up?" Bosco howled.

Thunder jumped up. "No mercy, Boz!" he yipped.

"Put him in a doggie bag!" Lightning added.

Bosco growled low in his throat, and suddenly all the dogs began barking loudly.

"Why are we barking?" Thunder demanded.

"I'm barking because you're barking!"

Lighting replied. "Why are you barking?"

Thunder barked louder. "I have no idea!"

Bosco crouched down, preparing to pounce on Marmaduke, baring his teeth.

"Bosco!" Jezebel snarled. "Stop!"

All the dogs stopped barking instantly, and Bosco's fury faded. Jezebel sauntered through the crowd, glaring at the other dogs, before stopping in front of Bosco.

"Relax, baby," Bosco said. "We're just horsin' around."

Thunder and Lightning struggled to stifle their giggles.

"No, you're not," Jezebel replied. "You're being a bully." She peered over at Marmaduke and Mazie. "I'm sorry, he gets this way when he drinks drainpipe water."

Mazie sniffed loudly. "That must be why you've dated him for two years." She turned to leave. "We're out of here."

Before Marmaduke could follow her, Bosco leaned close to whisper in his ear. "See you later when there aren't any girls around to save you," the muscular Beauceron hissed. "And Marmapup . . . ?"

Swallowing nervously, Marmaduke glanced back at Bosco.

"Next time I'll make you play dead," Bosco said. "Only I won't be playing."

Spooked, Marmaduke hurried to catch up to Mazie.

The mutts' walk in the darkness back to their neighborhood seemed very long. Marmaduke felt completely deflated as he trudged alongside Mazie, with Raisin and Giuseppe lagging a little behind.

"I'll never be able to show my face at the dog park again," Marmaduke whined.

"Those guys are jerks," Mazie replied. "They have no right to treat you like that."

Marmaduke hung his head. "Bosco's right about everything," he said. "I'm just a freak. I wasn't bred for anything but getting in the way. If I had a bone for every time someone said, 'Put a saddle on that thing,' or 'How's the weather up there?' I'd be a bone-illionaire. Just once in my life, I'd like to fit in, you know?"

"Look," Mazie said, "I know what it's like being an outsider." She glanced over at Marmaduke. "I was a rescue dog. Nobody wanted me.

You're better than any of those guys, and I can prove it. I can make you into the dog you want to be."

Marmaduke stopped short. "Really?" he asked. "Why would you do that for me?"

Mazie faced Marmaduke fully. "Because you're my friend."

For a long moment, Marmaduke stared at Mazie, but then he smiled warmly.

Just as Raisin and Giuseppe caught up to them, Marmaduke looked at the horizon and saw that the sun was coming up. "Wait, what time is it?" Marmaduke asked. "Phil's getting up soon—I gotta go!"

He took off running.

"You're welcome!" Mazie called indignantly after him.

The sun had fully risen by the time Marmaduke reached his house. He skidded across the lawn, ducked into the side yard, and zoomed through the doggie door in the back. Panting, he crept upstairs as quietly as he could, and tiptoed into the bedroom, where Debbie, Phil, and Carlos were still sleeping.

Marmaduke slipped into the bed and delicately

slid under Phil's arm. He let out a relieved sigh just as Phil's alarm went off.

Phil sat up and ruffled the fur on Marmaduke's head. "Ready to go to work, buddy?"

Blinking his tired eyes, Marmaduke sat up, too. "Just getting up," he barked.

After breakfast, Phil drove the car toward the park. He talked on his cell phone headset while Marmaduke lay in the backseat half asleep, groggily watching surfers in the ocean on the other side of the highway.

"I've got some great ideas percolating, Don," Phil said into his headset. "I just need a little more time to flesh them out." He gulped at something Don said. "No, you can count on me," he replied. "It's going to be a home run."

Phil disconnected the call and let out a big sigh, obviously struggling to come up with the idea Don demanded.

That's when Marmaduke saw the bee crawling on the inside of the backseat window.

Marmaduke sat up, his body tingling with panic. "Bee!" he barked. "Bee!"

"Marmaduke, quiet!" Phil ordered.

"Get him, Phil!" Marmaduke cried, jumping

to a standing position on the backseat. "I hate bees! Bees hate me!"

Phil pulled the car over and turned around to find out what was wrong with Marmaduke. Unnoticed by Phil or Marmaduke, the bee zoomed behind Phil's head and out the driver's side window. "Be quiet!" Phil told Marmaduke, then he spotted the guys on surfboards in the ocean outside, and he figured that was what had upset the dog. "They're just surfers."

As soon as he said those words, Phil froze, staring at the surfers in the waves. A smile twitched his lips as he was struck by an idea. "Marmaduke, you're a genius."

I am? Marmaduke wondered, still looking around for the bee.

A few minutes later, Phil was walking barefoot with Don through the dog meadow in the park. Phil pitched Don his idea.

Don stopped walking momentarily. "A surf competition for dogs?"

"Man's best friends surfing toward shore," Phil explained. "Throngs of owners cheering them on. Hilarious clips on the internet that we can use to create a viral web campaign."

Don didn't look convinced, but he started walking again, and Phil followed. "Yeah," Don said, "but dogs on surfboards? How's that going to sell organic dog food in the heartland? Three o'clock."

Phil glanced down at the lawn and side-stepped a meadow muffin. "If you want to sell to the Midwest, I'll tell you how—be true to who you are. Bark Organics was made in Southern California. Embrace that. Bring the iconic spirit of the West Coast to every dog owner across the country."

Tapping his lips with a finger, Don tilted his head to stare at Phil intently. "I hired you to create an identity for this company . . . and you say be yourself? We've got only one shot."

"I know we do," Phil replied. "You're going to have to trust me."

Don looked deeply into Phil's eyes for a long, searching moment. Finally, he nodded. "Okay, one shot," he said. "Make it happen."

Phil smiled proudly as Don strode away, but then he noticed something on the grass. "Look out!" Phil shouted.

Flailing his arms, Don ducked and covered

his head. "Where?" he hollered.

"Just a meadow muffin!" Phil called. He pointed near Don's feet. "Right there."

Don smiled sheepishly. "I thought you were talking about your dog."

Shaking his head, Phil pointed across the dog meadow. "No, he's way over there."

Marmaduke was hanging with Mazie near the large pond. Mazie put Pig Cow down between Marmaduke's feet. "Okay," she said, "your mutt makeover begins now. First things first, Pig Cow is yours—a big confidence booster. Chew on him if you get nervous."

"Thanks," Marmaduke said.

"Next, let's smell that breath," Mazie said. She took a whiff . . . and gasped. "Whoa, that needs work! Peds have dental hygienists, so garbage breath's not gonna fly. Stay out of trash cans and eat more mint-based items."

Marmaduke nodded. "Less trash, more mint. Check."

"Next, stand up proud," Mazie instructed, standing up tall herself. "Your ancestors sat at the foot of kings, man. Let's put the Great back in Dane here."

After shaking himself, Marmaduke straightened as high as he could raise himself. He lifted his head up, and suddenly he looked very different from his usual slouchy self. Marmaduke actually looked regal.

Mazie gulped, impressed by his new posture. "Uh," she said, trying not to let her enthusiasm show, "and your ears, uh, maybe keep your ears up, too."

"Like this?" Marmaduke asked, perking his ears up attentively.

"Yeah," Mazie agreed, starting to pant. "Definitely like that."

Marmaduke's ears perked up even higher when he noticed Jezebel sauntering by on the far side of the meadow. "Uh, just out of curiosity," he asked Mazie, "do you think any of this stuff would work with . . . girls?"

Mazie stopped panting, and her shoulders slumped. "Oh," she said sadly, "you mean with Jezebel."

"Not specifically," Marmaduke said, trying to sound offhand. "Just thinking out loud here."

Mazie turned away from Marmaduke and stared out at the ducks swimming in circles in the middle of the pond. She sighed softly. "Okay, listen up, Barkanova," she said. "I can only speak for myself here, but if you really want to impress a girl, you've got to take her on her dream date."

Marmaduke blinked at her blankly.

"You have no idea how to do that," Mazie said, "do you?"

"No," Marmaduke answered honestly.

"Well," Mazie said, "if it were me, I'd want him to take me to the junkyard. It's really romantic there at night." Her eyes glazed over dreamily as she imagined the scene. "There'd be a blanket with some treats spread out. Music from an old car radio would be playing softly—"

"Flat tires and broken windows," Marmaduke said excitedly, wagging his tail. "Where do I make reservations?"

Mazie shook her head. "You've got so much to learn," she told him. "Girls want romance, mystery. Tell her that her collar's pretty. Walk around her a few times."

"Okay," Marmaduke replied, nodding. "You want me to try on you?"

Mazie swallowed, surprised by the offer, but she tried to play it cool, even ignoring the sound of an approaching ambulance's siren. "Uh, yeah," she said. "You know, sure."

Marmaduke started to circle Mazie. But Mazie whirled around to face him.

They stared deeply into each other's eyes. Mazie felt paralyzed by his gaze.

"What?" she asked, breaking the silence.

"You know," Marmaduke said softly, "I never really noticed before . . . but you have really pretty—"

His sentence was interrupted by the ambulance roaring past the park, its siren wailing loudly. Except for Mazie, all the dogs in the park started howling . . . including Marmaduke. "Owwww!" he bellowed. "Owwwwwww!"

"Hey," Mazie protested. "We're talking here."

"Oh, sorry," Marmaduke said, breaking off his howl. "Where were we?"

Mazie blushed. "You said I have really pretty—"

Before she could finish, Phil hurried over and clipped Marmaduke's leash onto his collar. "Gotta go, buddy!" he said. "Work to do."

Marmaduke strained against the leash. "Wait, Phil!" he barked. "I need . . . that." He grabbed

Pig Cow in his jaws, and Phil pulled him away from Mazie.

"Really pretty what?" Mazie called after him.

"What?" Marmaduke barked back, his word muffled by the toy in his mouth.

By then he was too far away to hear Mazie if she repeated her question, so she just stared after him wistfully, watching him go.

CHAPTER 5

When Phil and Marmaduke arrived home, Phil opened the back gate and Marmaduke barreled inside, rushing over to greet Debbie.

Debbie was talking to a tall stranger in the backyard, and Marmaduke sniffed him. He smelled self-assured and faintly like cheese.

"Honey," Debbie said to Phil, while patting Marmaduke on the head, "the new dog trainer you think we need is here."

Marmaduke narrowed his eyes at the trainer while Phil shook his hand.

"Hi, Phil Winslow," Phil introduced himself.

The trainer bowed slightly. "I am Anton, master of the Top Dog Method," he replied. "And you are late, Winston."

"It's Winslow," Phil corrected him.

Anton sniffed haughtily. "That's what I said."

Really? Marmaduke thought, trying not to laugh. *I'm supposed to listen to a guy named Anton?*

"Okay," Phil said amicably. "Well, basically we just need some help here with Marmaduke. Sometimes he's a little hard to control, and he doesn't always listen—"

"Would you like to run this?" Anton interrupted. "Or shall I?"

Phil raised his hands. "Go ahead."

"Do you allow your dog to share your bed?" asked Anton.

"It's our bed," Marmaduke barked.

"Well," Phil began, "actually . . ."

Anton put his hands on his hips. "It's a yes-or-no question."

"Yeah," Phil answered.

Anton pursed his lips. "Do you give him snacks or allow him to eat human food from the table?"

"Does pizza count?" Marmaduke barked worriedly.

"He does like waffles," Debbie replied.

Anton raised his eyebrows at her. "It's easier if I just speak to one person," he said curtly. "Thank you."

"We're trying to—" Phil started to argue, raising a finger.

"Yes," Anton broke in, "or no?"

Phil lowered his finger. "Yes," he said.

"Does your dog obey simple commands?" asked Anton.

Debbie and Phil glanced at each other, but neither responded.

Anton stepped closer to Phil. "Of course not," he said. "It's obvious where the problem is here."

"Hang on," Phil said. He pointed to Marmaduke. "He's the problem."

"I'm the problem?" Marmaduke barked.

Anton shook his head. "You think your dog is the problem? Observe." He circled around Marmaduke and carefully crouched until his lips were level with the dog's ear. "Let me in, Marmaduke," he whispered. "I'm your friend. I'm going to help you."

Why is he whispering? Marmaduke wondered.

Debbie leaned over and whispered to Phil, "Why is he whispering?"

Anton glared at Debbie. "Could I have a bit of quiet, please? I'm talking to a dog!" He stood up and pointed at Marmaduke. "Stay," he ordered.

Confused, Marmaduke remained standing where he was.

Anton nodded, satisfied. "You see how the canine behaves with me?" he asked. "There is no question as to who is the leader and who is the follower." He pointed at Marmaduke again. "Marmaduke, sit! Sit . . . sit . . . sit!"

Marmaduke didn't budge.

That's when little Sarah walked into the backyard. She smiled. "Marmaduke," she said, "sit!"

Marmaduke sat down.

Anton shot Sarah a nasty look, which only made the little girl giggle. "You," he spat at Sarah, "you're not helping. Not one bit."

"She's three," Phil said in Sarah's defense.

"Well, that's twenty-one in dog years!" argued Anton. He waved his hand dismissively. "You see, he sits! Anton has dominance! Anton is the Top Dog!"

I've got chills, Marmaduke thought sarcastically.

Anton glared at Phil. "Your problem, Winston," he said, "is that you've enabled your dog to have free range over your house and your life. You don't own him, he owns you. It's time to take back control. Are you ready to become Top Dog?"

"Sure," Phil replied with a shrug.

Anton pointed down at the grass in front of Marmaduke. "On your belly, facing the trainee," he ordered.

Phil shook his head. "I'm sorry, but I don't think—"

"Phil?" Anton interrupted.

"Yes," Phil said.

Anton whipped a small water bottle out of a holster on his belt and sprayed Phil in the face.

"Ah!" Phil hollered. "What'd you do that for?"

"To get your attention," replied Anton.

Phil wiped his eyes. "I was already paying—"

Anton sprayed him in the face again.

"Stop it!" Phil gasped. "Is that necessary?"

Anton nodded. "I've trained difficult dogs, Phil," he said. "Hollywood dogs. If you want an obedient animal, lie down and don't question the Top Dog Method."

"Okay," Phil said. "Just don't spray me again."

"I can't promise that," said Anton.

Reluctantly, Phil spread himself out flat on his stomach, face-to-face with Marmaduke. Anton kneeled beside Phil.

Maybe I was a bit quick to judge Anton, Marmaduke thought. *This is great!*

"In order for Marmaduke to respect you in your world," Anton explained, "you must enter his and show him who's Top Dog. Gain his trust, then betray it. Do that and he'll respect you forever."

"How do I do that?" Phil asked. "I'm not questioning the method. It's just a regular question."

Anton pressed a hand over his heart. "It works by trusting and obeying the expert, Phil," he said. "Now roll onto your back, extremities in the air."

With a sigh, Phil did as he was told, raising his limbs. Debbie and Sarah chuckled.

I totally underestimated Anton, thought

Marmaduke. *I've never seen Phil behave so well.*

"Now repeat after me," Anton told Phil. "'Hey, Marmaduke . . . let's play!'"

"Hey, Marmaduke," Phil repeated. "Let's play."

"More enthusiasm!" Anton ordered. "Wriggle around! Say, 'I love to play, ha ha! I love to get tackled and wrestle!'"

"Um," said Phil. "Ha ha! I love to play! I love to get tackled and wrestle!"

Anton suddenly tossed a dog snack onto Phil's chest.

Instinctively, Marmaduke leaped onto the treat.

"Now betray him!" Anton insisted. "Show him who's Top Dog!"

Phil struggled to flip Marmaduke over, but the big dog was too heavy to move. Marmaduke lay down on top of Phil and comfortably munched on the treat.

Anton shuffled closer to Phil's head. "Not bad for your first try," he said. "How does it feel?"

"Awkward," Phil answered. "Confusing. Mostly awkward and confusing."

Anton nodded. "Two weekly lessons for three

months should clear that right up."

"Three months?" asked Phil, shocked.

Anton pulled out his water bottle again and spritzed Phil in the face.

Marmaduke swallowed his treat and chuckled. *I love dog training,* he thought.

That night, Marmaduke stood in the upstairs hallway bathroom, staring at himself in the mirror with his front paws on the sink. Carlos sat curled up on the closed toilet lid.

After pawing at a tube of toothpaste to move it closer, Marmaduke chomped down on the tube. Sticky toothpaste spewed around the bathroom.

"Dude, watch it!" Carlos complained. "I just gave myself a tongue bath!"

Marmaduke smeared the toothpaste around the inside of his mouth with his tongue and dropped down from the sink. He leaned over to Carlos and panted on him. "How's my breath?"

Carlos sniffed. "Refreshingly minty."

With a nod, Marmaduke propped himself back up on the sink. He practiced perking up his ears in the mirror and then attempted to raise his posture again.

"Who am I kidding?" he groaned, slumping. "Minty breath, better posture . . . this stuff will never work. Those guys have skills. I could never speak Gopher."

Carlos licked one of his paws. "Breaking into new cliques is tough," he said. "But why would you want to speak Gopher?"

Marmaduke ignored the question, too preoccupied with wanting to impress the peds . . . and Jezebel. "I don't get it," he said. "I'm a dog and you're a cat, and we get along great."

"That's because you're my *hermano*," Carlos answered. He flexed his paw, exposing his sharp claws. "If we weren't related, I'd scratch both your eyes out."

Marmaduke barked a laugh. "You could never take me," he shot back. "I'd cream your furry little—"

He stopped, struck by an idea. He smiled at the cat. "Carlos, you're a genius."

Carlos's tail twitched nervously. "Nuh-uh," he said. "No way. I know that look and I don't like it."

Marmaduke didn't stop grinning.

"This is going to cost you at least three cans

M
armaduke and his family moved to a new city,

MARMADUKE

so he hopes he can make some
new friends at the dog park.

He meets
Raisin, who is
really smart;

Giuseppe,
who is always
a little nervous;

and Mazie, who
wants to help
Marmaduke fit in.

But he also meets some pedigreed dogs at the park, and they're not very nice.

Bosco is their leader, and Jezebel is his girlfriend.

Marmaduke fakes a fight with
a cat to impress the pedigrees.

It works so well he becomes their leader.

He even starts dating Jezebel!

This calls for a party, complete with toilet water for everyone!

Marmaduke is on top of the world!

But what about his old friends? Does he still have time for them now that he's Top Dog?

of tuna," Carlos said. "And you gotta tell me where Debbie hid the catnip."

The next morning, Marmaduke put his plan into action. He entered the park, holding his head up high as he walked confidently toward the shady spot where the pedigreed dogs hung out.

When he reached them, Marmaduke loudly cleared his throat. "Say, does anyone smell that?" he asked. He ignored the peds' blank stares. "I smell a cat. And I hate cats."

Marmaduke glanced at a grove of nearby bushes. Nothing happened.

Bosco glared at Marmaduke, who gulped. "I simply can't comprehend how dense you are," Bosco snarled. "What are you doing over here, Rin Tin Ton?"

"Uh," Marmaduke repeated desperately, "I said I smell a cat!"

Carlos suddenly tumbled out of the bushes, landing awkwardly on the lawn near the dogs. "Ouch!" he groaned. The cat scrambled to his feet. "Oh, where am I?" he said, his acting rather wooden. "Is this a dog park? I must be horribly lost."

The pedigreed dogs began to growl, their hackles rising.

Marmaduke stepped in between the peds and Carlos. "This one's mine, fellas," he told the dogs. He sneered at Carlos. "Yeah, you must be lost, cat," he said coldly. "This park is for dogs only."

"Please don't hurt me, mister," Carlos mewed. "I'm just a poor, incredibly attractive, ultra-intelligent cat who has lost his way."

Marmaduke crouched down in pouncing position. "You're about to lose something else, too," he replied. "Your dignity!"

"Fight!" cheered Lightning. "Fight!"

The peds gathered around Marmaduke and Carlos. Marmaduke even spotted Mazie, Raisin, and Giuseppe watching from a distance.

Carlos pretended to look scared. "You are the biggest, baddest dog I have ever seen in my life," he squealed. "You also seem cool and confident!"

"You're right about that," Marmaduke said, "you fish-eating freak."

With a tilt of his head, Carlos whispered, "I wish I ate more fish." Then he jumped back into character. "Please spare my life!"

"Spare this!" Marmaduke barked. He batted

Carlos gently with his paw, and Carlos faked a stumble that didn't look very convincing.

"Come on, sell it, man," Carlos hissed in a whisper. "Put some muscle into it."

"Okay, okay," Marmaduke whispered back. He stood up tall. "Get up!" he growled at Carlos. "I'm not through with you!"

Carlos hopped to his feet, and Marmaduke smacked him a little harder.

"That's more like it!" Carlos whispered.

Marmaduke swiped the cat again, whacking Carlos more forcefully. The peds cheered as Carlos staggered, wobbling on his paws.

"Okay," Carlos suggested softly, "maybe we could find a happy medium."

"Keep going," Marmaduke whispered. "It's working!"

Carlos squealed in fake terror. "No!" he shrieked. "Stop! You are too much dog for me to handle! So strong! So much effortless charisma!"

"Don't you ever forget it!" Marmaduke barked. Pumped up on adrenaline, he leaped onto Carlos and pummeled the cat hard.

The pedigreed dogs howled in approval.

"I weigh only eight pounds!" Carlos gasped

as Marmaduke whaled on him. "This officially hurts now! Stop!"

Marmaduke chomped down on Carlos's tail and hoisted him up in the air. Carlos screamed as Marmaduke swung him a few times and then flung him off to the side.

When Carlos landed, he glanced back at his tail. The fur along its entire length had been stripped off.

The peds woofed in laughter.

"What's the matter, Bigglesworth?" Marmaduke taunted. "Dog got your tongue?" He spat out a wad of wet fur.

Carlos stared at Marmaduke, his eyes filled with pain. "Whatever, man," he said. "I hope you got what you wanted."

Then Carlos turned around and dashed toward the bushes.

Marmaduke watched until the cat disappeared, realizing that he'd gone too far.

"That was hilarious!" Thunder cheered. "Way to go!"

"Not as good as Bosco," Lightning added, "but you schooled that fleabag!"

All the peds turned to look at Bosco,

wondering what he thought.

Bosco yawned. "Laughable," he muttered. He marched away, and the pedigreed dogs followed their leader.

Jezebel hung back. "You've got a keen sense of smell," she told Marmaduke.

"Thanks," Marmaduke replied. "Must be the large nostrils."

With a glance at Bosco, Jezebel raised her eyebrows. "I have to go," she said, "but . . . maybe I'll see you around."

"Cool," Marmaduke said. "I'd like that."

Jezebel started to walk toward the other peds, but after a few steps, she turned around. "Oh, and Marmaduke?" she called back. "Promise me you won't pick on any more cats, okay? The bully stuff doesn't really impress me." She twitched her nose. "I dig the minty breath, though." With a smile, Jezebel continued walking away.

Marmaduke grinned and then hustled over to Mazie, Raisin, and Giuseppe.

"What gives with the cat hazing?" Mazie demanded. "That's not what we worked on."

"She talked to me!" Marmaduke panted. "She liked my minty breath!"

Marmaduke raised his paw for Mazie to pound it, which she reluctantly did. Then he flipped over onto his back and squirmed around on the grass, thrilled with the way his plan had worked.

Mazie stared at him, a worried expression shadowing her eyes.

CHAPTER 6

The next Saturday, Phil stood in the middle of Huntington Beach, directing pedestrian traffic. A banner on poles above Phil read, BARK ORGANICS 1ST ANNUAL DOG SURFING CONTEST. COWABARKA! The beach behind him was busy with dogs, their owners, and people arriving to enjoy the show.

"Two minute countdown, everyone!" Phil shouted. "Owners and dogs, make your way to the shore!"

With a good view of the surfing area, Debbie sat under an umbrella doing an impossible crossword puzzle. Not far away, Marmaduke was digging a deep hole in the sand.

Phil spotted Don heading his way, wearing sunglasses and a hat. He was leading two serious-looking executives, a man and a woman, both in full business suits. Phil dragged Marmaduke out of the hole and pulled him toward Don.

As Phil approached, Don introduced him to the executives. "And this is our division marketing manager, Phil Winslow. Phil, these are David King and Jessica Frankel, with the largest pet store chain in the country."

Phil shook the pet store executives' hands. "Pleased to meet you both," he said. "I hope you're ready for a mind-blowing canine surfing experience."

Jessica couldn't take her eyes off Marmaduke. "Wow," she said, amazed by his size. "I can't wait to see this big guy out on the waves." She and David laughed heartily.

What? Marmaduke thought worriedly. *Nuh-uh. No way. You should see me in the bathtub! It's hopeless.*

"Actually," Don said, "Phil and Marmaduke are only a month removed from Kansas. They're probably not ready to hang twenty yet."

David adjusted his tie. "That's too bad," he said, shaking his head. "Seems like it would've been the big home run everyone's looking for."

Phil couldn't let the pet store people be disappointed by his Bark Organics event. "Of course, Don's just being modest," he said quickly. "Marmaduke and I would love to swing for the fences."

"You would?" Don gasped, his eyes wide with surprise.

"We would?" Marmaduke barked.

"Surf's up!" Phil said, pumping his fist weakly. He smiled at Marmaduke.

Marmaduke stared flatly at Phil. *We're dead,* he thought.

A few minutes later, Phil was outfitted in a wetsuit and given a surfboard to use. He and Marmaduke stood on the shoreline, staring worriedly out at the waves.

A loudspeaker squawked behind them. "And in our final weight class," an announcer cried, "give it up for SoCal surf champs, Ron Anderson and Bosco!"

Marmaduke turned to see Bosco and his muscular owner walk past them to the ocean. Bosco's owner put his surfboard down in the water, and Bosco hopped aboard.

"See you in the drink, Shamu!" Bosco called

back to Marmaduke.

"Good luck to you, too," Marmaduke dead-panned. "I never would've guessed in a million years you'd be my competition."

Bosco's owner paddled the surfboard out into deeper water.

The loudspeaker squawked again. "And let's give a big hand to Phil Winslow and Marmaduke!" the announcer shouted.

The audience applauded as Phil gave them a nervous wave.

Debbie hurried over to Phil. "Are you sure you want to do this, honey?"

"Yeah," Phil said. He glanced over at Don, who was staring at him intently. "It's going to be great."

Then Phil noticed that Marmaduke was slinking away, keeping his body low to the sand. Phil ran after him, grabbed his collar, and tried to pull him back toward the starting area, but Marmaduke didn't budge. "Come!" Phil ordered. "Top Dog says, 'Come!'"

"No way!" Marmaduke barked. "Marmie don't surf!"

Phil and Marmaduke struggled for a moment

more, until Marmaduke suddenly froze. He had spotted Jezebel sashaying along the beach. She had her long fur done in beautiful braids with beads that twinkled mesmerizingly in the sunlight. When she saw Marmaduke staring at her, she winked.

Marmaduke gulped. He was stuck in the classic situation: between a rock and a hard place. He realized that he could either be a coward or suck it up and impress the hottest girl on the beach. It was the kind of situation that defined someone as a hero, and it was time to be that hero.

Raising his head high, Marmaduke faced the ocean bravely. He strode confidently toward the water and leaped into the surf.

Marmaduke immediately jumped back out. "That's cold!" he howled.

But he didn't give up. In moments, he was clinging nervously to the surfboard as it bobbed up and down on gentle swells.

Phil stood chest-deep in the water beside Marmaduke, trying to steady the surfboard. "Stay, Marmaduke," he said soothingly, "it's okay. Nothing bad is going to happen."

Oh, something bad is going to happen, Phil,

Marmaduke thought darkly. *Payback's going to hurt.*

Bosco's owner paddled their surfboard close to Marmaduke. To Marmaduke's surprise, Bosco made the sound of a ringing phone. "I need to take this," he said, and he raised his paw to his ear, pretending to answer the call. "Bosco speaking. Oh, hello again, old friend! Don't worry, I've got this thing wrapped up." He hung up his imaginary phone and smirked at Marmaduke. "That was destiny calling. Excuse me, it's my time to dazzle."

With a grunt, Bosco's owner pushed their surfboard into the crest of a turning wave. Bosco steered the board with his paws, catching the wave beautifully. The Beauceron even managed to stand up on his hind legs for a moment, hot-dogging for the cheering crowd.

Marmaduke glanced at Phil, who looked as intimidated as he felt. They both stared at a wave that was gaining strength as it approached.

"Okay," Phil asked, "you ready?"

"No!" barked Marmaduke. "No! Help!"

"Go!" Phil shouted.

Marmaduke braced himself on the surfboard.

"Tell Debbie I loved her sandwiches!" he howled.

Phil pushed the surfboard into place to catch the wave. The curl caught Marmaduke's board, and he managed to remain standing for about five seconds before the surfboard suddenly jerked to an abrupt stop. Marmaduke toppled into the water and splashed around as Phil quickly swam over to him.

"Sorry," Phil said, holding up the strap that was attached to his wrist . . . and the back of the surfboard. "I forgot to take the leash off."

Marmaduke paddled frantically in the water. "Get me out!" he barked. "Out!"

But despite his panic and shakiness, Marmaduke still didn't give up. He tried again with the next wave, and the next, and the one after that. Even though he wiped out horribly each time, he also improved a little bit, slowly getting the feel for balancing himself on the surfboard.

Marmaduke was resting on his board, wet and shivering, enjoying a brief phase of calmer water, when Bosco and his owner paddled over to him again.

"How are you holding up, Loch Ness?"

Bosco asked nastily.

Happy thoughts, Marmaduke reminded himself. *I'm running through a meadow, peeing on everything. . . .*

Phil glanced back toward the beach, where Don and the executives were watching him. He faced the ocean, his jaw set firmly. Bosco's owner and Phil spotted the upcoming giant wave at the same time. It was twice as big as any other wave they'd seen all day. "You gotta be kidding me," Phil muttered.

"Too big!" Marmaduke barked. "Not ready!"

"Hold on, Marmaduke!" Phil hollered. He and Bosco's owner both shoved their surfboards toward the humongous wave.

Bosco and Marmaduke both caught the wave, which was barreling toward shore at a frightening speed. For a moment, the dogs surfed side by side.

"Off my wave, poser!" Bosco shouted.

Marmaduke stumbled slightly on his board, and the surfboard veered wildly, accidentally cutting off Bosco just as the wave began to curl.

Bosco wiped out, flipping off his board into the water.

As the wave curled into a wide tube, Marmaduke somehow kept his balance on the board. He ripped through the curl, the ocean's roar in the noisy tube echoing in his ears. Marmaduke's legs trembled, and he almost teetered off the board, but then he looked down at his paws. He suddenly felt filled with surprising confidence, and he shifted his balance back over the board, spreading out his toes.

Marmaduke looked up, raising his chin in determination. *You can do this,* he told himself. *You have the power inside you to shred. Your ancestors sat at the foot of kings. You are . . . slipping off the board!*

His surfboard shot out of the tube, slicing across the face of the wave. Marmaduke scrambled to stay on the board, terror making him wriggle awkwardly as he tried everything he could to keep upright.

Thinking he was shredding the wave, the crowd cheered. They hollered louder when Marmaduke accidentally made his board spin around.

Then Marmaduke wiped out completely, landing with a loud splash in the ocean.

When he surfaced, he spat out saltwater and stumbled onto the sand, covered with seaweed. Phil hurried out of the ocean and plopped down beside him, giving Marmaduke a big, wet hug.

Panting, Marmaduke was surprised when a crowd of cheering dogs surrounded him.

"That was off the hook, dude!" a Jack Russell barked.

An Irish setter jumped up and down. "Totally epic!"

"You rule, man!" a bulldog bayed.

Marmaduke grinned at them, starting to enjoy the attention.

At the end of the competition, Phil led Marmaduke up on a stage that had been set up on the sand, where Bosco and his owner already waited. Don stood on the stage with the pet store executives. On the other side were a few small dogs wearing ribbons they had won. Behind the executives was a table with a tall trophy on it, which was shaped like a dog surfing on a bone. Next to the trophy was a big punch bowl and a tray with refreshments.

Don stepped up to the microphone. "Before announcing Bark Organics's Large Dog Surf

Champion," he announced, "I'd like to take this opportunity to thank our very talented dogs, who enrich our lives in so many countless ways. Heck, they're the reason we're all out here getting sunburned today. Thank you, dogs, one and all."

While the audience applauded, Bosco leaned over to Marmaduke. "You think it was funny dropping in on my wave like that, Marmapuke?"

"Let it go, Bosco," Marmaduke replied. "It was an accident."

Don adjusted the microphone, and it screeched with feedback. "And now," he announced, "the award for Large Dog Surf Champion goes to . . ." He smiled and pulled out an envelope with a flourish.

Marmaduke leaned closer to Bosco. "Now that you mention it," he growled, "yeah, I did think it was funny. Your girlfriend did, too."

"It's an upset!" Don called out. "Phil and Marmaduke Winslow!"

Phil looked down at Marmaduke, and Marmaduke gazed up at him, both their eyes wide with surprise. The crowd cheered wildly.

Bosco went ballistic, barking and bucking his body up and down. "You're dead, mutt!" he screamed at Marmaduke. Then Bosco lunged at Marmaduke, his teeth bared.

Marmaduke backed up and smacked into the refreshment table. The big trophy toppled over and hit the punch bowl, which flipped into the air, drenching the pet store executives with pink juice.

With a furious growl, Bosco chased Marmaduke around the stage, under the table, and between people. Marmaduke whacked into the podium, knocking it over. Bosco barreled into folding chairs, which snapped shut with a clatter. People screamed as the stage wobbled and banners floated down to the sand.

Bosco cornered Marmaduke against the executives' legs—they were backed up, terrified, against the rear wall of the stage. As Bosco approached, snarling, Marmaduke narrowed his eyes and raised his head high.

Not this time, he thought firmly.

Marmaduke suddenly leaped forward and growled at Bosco, showing the smaller dog all his sharp, huge teeth.

Surprised, Bosco stepped backward . . . and cowered submissively.

Silence fell over the stage. Marmaduke looked up and saw that all the people and dogs were staring at him quietly. Bosco, humiliated, slunk off the stage.

"No!" Phil scolded, grabbing Marmaduke by the collar. "Stop it! Bad boy!" He faced the executives, his cheeks red with embarrassment. "I'm so sorry about this."

Don put his hand on Phil's shoulder. A torn banner was draped around Don's shoulders, and there was sand in his hair. "You'd better get your dog under control," Don growled, showing his white teeth. "Understand?"

Phil nodded, and Don walked off the stage.

After all the mess had been cleaned up, Phil huddled by a bonfire on the beach, looking tired as he watched the sunset over the ocean. Debbie sat down beside him. "You okay?" she asked softly.

Phil sighed. "What's a nine-letter word that means 'destroys everything in its path'?"

"Don Twombly?" Debbie guessed, half-joking. "No, wait, that's ten."

"You know exactly who I'm talking about," Phil replied tightly.

Debbie rubbed Phil's shoulder. "Look, sweetie," she said, "we've been here almost a month, and this is the first time we've even been to the beach—and it was for work. Let's relax and recharge. Maybe take some time for the family next weekend. What do you say?"

Phil glanced over at her. After a second, his face relaxed a little and he let himself smile. "I say yes."

Leaning against him, Debbie smiled, too.

Down the beach, Marmaduke was sitting alone by the waterline, enjoying the breeze making his ears flutter. He looked up when he heard the tinkle of Jezebel's beaded braids.

"Hey," Jezebel asked, stepping closer to him. "What are you doing by yourself?"

"Hey," Marmaduke said. "I'm just taunting some sand crabs. They think I'm Godzilla." He stood up and pretended to stomp on invisible crabs.

Jezebel laughed. "You're funny."

"Actually," Marmaduke admitted, "I was just taking a break from my family. We're kind of having a rough stretch."

"I know the feeling," Jezebel replied. She was quiet a moment, and then said, "I thought you were pretty gutsy out there today."

Marmaduke raised his eyebrows. "Really?"

"Consider me very impressed," Jezebel said. She shivered and shifted closer to Marmaduke. "It's getting a little cold out," she whispered. She rested her head against his neck and nuzzled him.

"Wait," said Marmaduke. "What about Bosco?"

Jezebel sniffed loudly. "Forget about him," she said. "There's a new dog in town, one with a little class. And his name is Marmaduke."

Marmaduke cocked his head at her. "Hey, that's my name," he said. He met her eyes, and they looked meaningfully at each other. Then Jezebel leaned forward and gave him a peck on the cheek.

Marmaduke felt like he was in heaven.

CHAPTER 7

The next day, Anton arrived for another training session. Debbie and the kids sat down on patio chairs in the backyard to watch.

Phil stood by the pool, holding a rubber bone, which Marmaduke kept staring at very attentively. Anton hovered nearby, his spray bottle out and ready.

Gonna get the bone, Marmaduke thought. *Gonna get the bone!*

"Show him who's boss!" Anton told Phil. "Top Dog him!"

Phil pretended to throw the bone, but never let it out of his hand. "Go get it!" he shouted at Marmaduke.

Marmaduke galloped onto the grass, searching desperately for the rubber bone. *Where is it?*

he wondered. *Where did it go?* He stopped and glanced back at Phil, who looked smug. *He didn't throw it, did he? I can't believe I fell for that! I'm not going to get burned next time, no way.*

After trotting back to Phil, Marmaduke sat and stared at the bone again.

Once again, Phil pretended to throw it, and Marmaduke took off like a shot.

Where is it? Marmaduke thought, sniffing the grass. *I don't see it.* Then he lowered his head grumpily. *I fell for it again. I hate this!*

"Great Top Dogging, Phil!" Anton cheered. He popped a little treat into Phil's mouth and patted his hair.

Phil shifted uncomfortably, feeling weirded out. "I have to say," he admitted, "it feels pretty good."

"Believe it!" Anton said. "Feel it. Say it loud: 'I'm Top Dog!'"

"I'm Top Dog," Phil repeated quietly.

"Louder!" Anton insisted.

Phil raised his voice slightly. "I'm Top Dog!"

Anton shook his head. "Pump your fists triumphantly in the air!" he bellowed. "And declare it to the world!"

After taking a deep breath, Phil raised his fists and shook them above his head. He was still holding the bone. "I am Top Dog!" he shouted.

"Top Dog this!" Marmaduke howled. He leaped for the bone in Phil's hand and smacked into Phil, who toppled backward into the pool.

That afternoon, Marmaduke sat in the shade of the palm trees in the dog park, in what used to be Bosco's spot. He was surrounded by the pedigreed dogs, and Jezebel sat right next to him. They all joked around and laughed, and Marmaduke was loving the attention. Thunder and Lightning were really funny once he had gotten to know them.

Mazie, Raisin, and Giuseppe approached the peds. "We're having a game night tomorrow," Mazie told Marmaduke, ignoring the snickers of Lightning and Thunder behind her. "It would be great if you could come."

"The peds are having a thing at the yacht club," Marmaduke replied coolly, "so I'm going to chill there awhile." He yawned. "Maybe I'll stop by after." He returned to joking around with the peds, ignoring the mutts.

The mutts stood there awkwardly for a

long moment, but eventually they walked away dejectedly.

Marmaduke sneaked a glance after them, but he quickly went back to laughing with his new friends.

The next morning, Marmaduke entered the kitchen to find Carlos eating breakfast from his bowl. Carlos glanced up at him, his face betraying no emotion whatsoever.

Marmaduke stepped up beside him to eat out of his own bowl. "'Sup," he greeted the cat. "Tail's looking better."

Carlos replied with nothing but chilly silence.

"Come on," Marmaduke said. "We're bros, remember?"

With an annoyed flick of his bald tail, Carlos turned and walked away.

Marmaduke just shrugged and finished his breakfast.

That night, Mazie glanced up at the clock in her garage. It read 11:45 P.M. . . . and Marmaduke still hadn't shown up. Raisin and Giuseppe were listlessly playing a game.

Mazie went to the half-open garage door and

peered outside. There was no sign of Marmaduke anywhere. He wasn't coming.

With a sigh, Mazie went back to watch Giuseppe beat Raisin at the game.

Instead of going to Mazie's party, Marmaduke had taken Jezebel to the junkyard. He led her on a moonlit path between heaps of rusty cars. She was keeping her eyes closed.

"How much farther?" Jezebel asked. "I can't take the suspense!"

"Almost there," Marmaduke replied, nudging her forward until she was exactly where he wanted her. "Okay, you can open them now. Hit it, boys!"

As Jezebel opened her eyes, the headlights of an old car flickered on, illuminating a large blanket on the ground. The blanket was covered with piles of dog biscuits, bowls of water, and different kinds of foods. She gasped in pleasure.

"Wait," Marmaduke said. "There's more."

He nodded his head toward the car, where Thunder and Lightning were waiting in the front seat. Seeing the signal, Thunder bit the radio knob and turned it. Pretty, old-fashioned romantic music drifted through the junkyard.

Jezebel smiled as Marmaduke led her toward the blanket.

"This way, madame," Marmaduke said formally. "How about a peanut butter appetizer?"

"My favorite," Jezebel replied with a giggle.

When they reached the blanket, Marmaduke and Jezebel each buried their noses in separate peanut butter jars. They licked blobs of the sticky goop off their lips.

"You really pulled out all the stops," said Jezebel. "It's very romantic."

Marmaduke sat down on the blanket. "I couldn't think of another girl I'd rather share it with."

"It's so creative, too," Jezebel said, looking around at the junkyard scene. "How did you ever think of this?"

Marmaduke shrugged. "It's just the kind of guy I am." He looked seriously into Jezebel's eyes. "Listen," he whispered, "I just wanted to say something. I wanted to say—"

A loud car honk interrupted him. The sudden sound made both Marmaduke and Jezebel jump, startled.

"Sorry!" Lighting called from the old car. "I

slipped off the seat!"

Marmaduke licked a glob of leftover peanut butter off his chin and returned to looking seriously at Jezebel. "I wanted to say that hanging out with you these last few weeks . . . which in dog years feels like months . . . it's like the first time in my life I feel like I really belong."

Touched by his thoughtful words, Jezebel leaned closer, batting her long eyelashes.

Marmaduke kissed her sweetly.

From an old car in the darkness across from Lightning and Thunder, Mazie watched Marmaduke and Jezebel kiss. Her stomach twisted sadly, and she had to sniffle quietly to keep from crying.

Then Mazie caught a glimpse of herself in the car's broken rearview mirror. Her fur was clumped and matted, and it looked like she could use a bath. Mazie didn't like the tomboy she saw in the mirror.

With a last glance at Marmaduke kissing Jezebel, Mazie jumped out of the old car and ran home.

The next afternoon, Marmaduke trotted along beside Phil as he walked in the dog park with Don. Both Phil and Don were barefoot.

"We're lucky," Don said. "They want us to revise the proposal."

Phil nodded, relieved. "No problem," he said. "I'll start working on it immediately."

Don shook his head. "There's too much riding on this for you to go solo. Ten o'clock."

Phil jumped to the side, narrowly missing stepping on a meadow muffin.

"I want you to come out to my boat this weekend," Don continued. "We'll both work on it."

"This weekend?" Phil asked. "My family and I were going to spend a little quality time together—"

"Don't worry," Don interrupted. "The family's invited. They can relax while we work."

Phil nodded. "Okay, I guess that would be—"

"Perfect," Don said.

They walked quietly for a little while, until Marmaduke started straining at his leash. Phil unhooked Marmaduke's collar, and Marmaduke ran off toward the pedigreed dogs under the palm trees.

"Now, unfortunately my wife insists that the

boat be dog free," Don explained. "It's outrageous, but I think she's jealous."

"Well," Phil said, "Jezebel is a beautiful dog."

Don glanced at him and then lowered his head awkwardly for a long moment. Finally, he looked up at Phil again. "So, how's the move coming along? You guys all settled in?"

"Oh, yeah," Phil replied. "We love the place. We couldn't imagine living anywhere else."

Don stuck his hands in his pockets. "Moving can be quite traumatic," he said quietly. "Wouldn't want to have to go through that again."

Phil and Don wandered past Raisin, Giuseppe, and Mazie, who were staring at Marmaduke playing with the peds. Thunder and Lightning were jumping over Marmaduke, although he had to lower himself slightly so they would make the leap.

"Look at him," Raisin said with a snort. "King of the park. Land shrimps at his beck and call."

Giuseppe looked up from gnawing on his own bald leg. "He went from the Great Mutt Hope to the Betrayer," he mumbled. "Don't tell him I said that, though."

Mazie sighed. "You guys have got to get over yourselves," she said. "You're sitting around complaining about a guy you barely know."

"Oh, your feelings aren't hurt?" Raisin asked. "Not even a little?"

"Of course not, don't be crazy," Mazie replied, raising her nose in the air.

Giuseppe raised his bushy white eyebrows. "Are you sure?"

"Of course I'm sure," Mazie said.

"Are you double-dog sure?" prodded Raisin.

Mazie glared at them and then stood up and stormed across the park toward the palms. Giuseppe and Raisin hurried to follow her.

When Mazie got close to the peds, Thunder and Lightning started barking wildly at her.

"Sit!" she ordered them.

They sat.

"You got it," Thunder said.

Lightning nodded. "Yes, ma'am."

Mazie pushed past them and strode over to Marmaduke, who was relaxing in the shade, surrounded by pedigreed dogs. Raisin and Giuseppe stood right behind her.

"Hey, guys," Marmaduke said calmly. "What's up?"

"You don't give a steaming pile about us anymore, so cut the act," Mazie snapped. "We took you in, we were your friends, but now you just sit over here and act like we're dirt!"

Marmaduke let out a short barking laugh. "What did they put in your kibble this morning?"

The peds around Marmaduke laughed, too.

Mazie's eyes started to well up with tears. "You . . . took her on my dream date," she said, her voice cracking. "How do you think that makes me feel?"

The peds made *oohing* and *ahhing* noises.

Before she started sobbing, Mazie whirled around and ran away.

"Bitter, party of one?" Lightning sniggered.

The pedigreed dogs laughed again—except for Marmaduke and Jezebel.

"What's the big deal?" Marmaduke asked. "We were just brainstorming ideas. You'd think she'd be thrilled that I used one."

Raisin stepped up to Marmaduke. "You don't get it, do you? She gave you Pig Cow! She likes you. At least she did until you turned your back on us and became a big phony-baloney sellout." He nodded toward Giuseppe. "I'm quoting him when I say that."

"Word," Giuseppe said.

Marmaduke hunched his shoulders in surprise. "She likes me?" he asked, feeling totally stunned. But then he saw the peds staring at him, and he relaxed again. "I mean, that's really cute and everything, but I already have a girlfriend." His gaze flickered toward Jezebel. "A pedigree girlfriend."

"So that's it?" Giuseppe asked.

Marmaduke shifted uncomfortably as everybody stared at him. Finally, he just shrugged. "Yeah," he replied. "I don't hang out with mutts anymore."

Hearing Marmaduke's harsh words made Raisin and Giuseppe wince, their eyes filled with hurt.

"That's your cue to head back to your side of the park, fellas," Lightning said.

"And here's a parting gift for you," added Thunder. He turned around and kicked grass all over Raisin and Giuseppe with his hind legs.

Raisin and Giuseppe nodded sadly, and walked away.

Marmaduke watched them go, feeling stricken with guilt.

The next Saturday morning was a busy one in the Winslow house, as the family got ready to go on Don's boat. Brian and Debbie hauled suitcases to the car while Phil went over his checklist again.

"Okay," he said, scanning his clipboard. "We got bathing suits, towels, sunglasses, fins, snorkels, inner tubes, water skis, and I've got to say, this is going to be pretty great spending the weekend together."

Barbara stepped in front of her father. "Dad, I'm begging you. Please let me stay at my friend's house so I can go to this party."

"Barbara," Phil replied calmly, "this is a family trip and you're coming with us."

With a dramatic sigh, Barbara flounced out the front door just as Debbie was coming back inside.

Phil pointed to Marmaduke, who was sitting placidly by the stairs. "Look how he just sits there," Phil said to Debbie. "You think the trainer's working?"

Debbie stuck her hand out to Phil. "Shake," she said.

Phil fumbled with his clipboard as he shook Debbie's hand.

"I think you're coming along great," she said, smiling.

Phil groaned and then looked suspiciously at Marmaduke again. "You think he'll be okay alone?"

Marmaduke made his face relax into his most angelic expression.

"He's got his food and water, and he can use the doggie door to go out on the lawn," Debbie said. "Laura down the street said she'd check on him a few times, too. He'll be fine."

Phil chuckled, nodding his head. "I mean," he said, "what's he going to do, invite his girl-friend over? Throw a party?"

Debbie laughed and walked out the front door to the car. A moment later, Phil followed her and shut the front door behind him.

As soon as the car pulled out of the drive-way, Marmaduke smiled broadly, thumping his tail happily.

CHAPTER 8

The party Marmaduke threw that night at the Winslows' would become legendary among dogs.

"Now this is an O.C. rager!" a Pomeranian cheered, as he entered the house with a dozen of his friends.

Hip-hop music blared at top volume out of the stereo. Pedigreed dogs filled the whole house, some dancing on the tabletops, some bouncing on the couch, all of them barking loudly as they partied hearty. They shredded pillows and peed in corners and raced in circles.

Jezebel and Marmaduke walked down the stairs and into the crowd as if they were the queen and king of the dog world. Marmaduke greeted each dog he passed.

"Looking good, Colby!" he told a German shepherd. "My boy, Topaz!" he called to a beagle. "Sweet collar, Aurora!" he complimented a nervous-looking Chihuahua.

Marmaduke reached the guest bathroom and stopped to peer inside. Thunder, Lightning, and a few other peds were cheering on Shasta, who was gulping water out of the toilet. "Chug! Chug!" the dogs chanted.

"Chug it, baby!" Marmaduke cried.

Lightning was standing on the toilet tank. He stumbled on the porcelain, knocking the seat down onto Shasta's head.

Shasta stumbled backward. "Not cool, dude!" he yelped.

"Sorry, dude!" Lightning shouted. "I slipped!"

Marmaduke laughed and continued on, passing a cocker spaniel who was dragging his butt on the carpet.

"It's so soothing," the cocker spaniel sighed.

"Feeling good, Gordy!" Marmaduke told him.

A panting, overexcited Chow Chow rushed up to Marmaduke. "Is this your party, dude?"

"Yes!" Marmaduke crowed.

"It's totally raging!" the Chow yelled. "I love it! I love you!" Then the Chow let out a long howl and fell over, passed out.

Jezebel and Marmaduke laughed. "You're a big hit, Top Dog," Jezebel said.

"Tell me something I don't know," Marmaduke replied. He pointed his muzzle toward the dance floor in the living room. "Let's shake a tail."

They hurried over and quickly started grooving to the music. Then, as the music swelled, they joined the dogs jumping on the couch and shredding pillows.

Outside, across the street, Mazie, Giuseppe, and Raisin sat on the sidewalk, forlornly watching Marmaduke partying. They could see him jumping up and down on the couch through the front window.

"Why does it seem like everyone is always having more fun than us?" Raisin asked.

"Because they are," Giuseppe answered. He sneezed loudly. "Great, now I'm catching a cold. I knew I should've worn my sweater."

Mazie stood up, fed up with watching the

party. "Come on, let's bail."

But then she stopped, sniffing the air. Her ears perked up.

"What do you smell, girl?" Raisin asked.

Mazie narrowed her eyes. "Trouble," she replied. She turned around slowly until she spotted a dog skulking across Marmaduke's front yard.

It was Bosco. He slipped around the corner of the house, keeping to the shadows as he entered the side yard.

Mazie glanced at Raisin and Giuseppe. All three of them looked very concerned.

Bosco met up with Carlos in the darkness, where the cat had been hiding from the partying dogs. "Do I know you from somewhere?" Bosco asked.

"Me?" Carlos replied, licking down the fur on one paw. "Nope. Never seen you before."

Bosco peered more closely at the cat. "You sure?" he asked. "That tail looks . . . painful."

"Of course I'm sure," Carlos said. "I've never even been to the dog park." He smiled. "Oops."

Inside, Marmaduke was back on the floor, boogying with Jezebel. The peds all circled around them, cheering as Marmaduke wriggled to the beat. He really hit his stride as the music reached a fever pitch, and the crowd went bonkers, barking and howling. Marmaduke felt like a star.

A loud crash—and the sudden cutting-off of the music—brought the party to a screeching halt.

Marmaduke looked over to see Bosco standing next to the broken music player on the floor. Carlos sat calmly beside the big Beauceron.

"Looks like a stellar party," Bosco growled. "Sorry to interrupt." He pointed at Carlos. "Quick question: Does anyone recognize this cute little fella?"

"*Hola,*" said Carlos. "Try the guacamole. It's dynamite."

All around Marmaduke, the peds began whispering to one another, and he started to feel concerned.

"Maybe he looks like a certain cat from the park that Marmaduke hazed?" Bosco continued. "Look at that tail. Well, it turns out that he lives here. With Marmaduke." He smiled nastily. "Or is it Marmafake?"

The peds all stared at Marmaduke, waiting

for an explanation.

Marmaduke swaggered toward Bosco. "You weren't invited here, so I think you should leave."

"Great comeback!" Bosco replied sarcastically. "I'm terrified. And I'm still waiting for an answer."

Puffing out his chest, Marmaduke stepped even closer to Bosco, glaring at him. "I don't answer to you," he said. "Leave now and you won't have a problem." He glanced down at Carlos. "And take Whiskers with you. We have a no-cat policy."

"Is that right?" Bosco asked. "Then how do you explain that picture in the foyer?"

Everyone turned to look toward the entrance hall, where a large photo of the Winslow family hung on the wall. In it, Marmaduke stood between Phil and Debbie, next to Barbara, Brian, and Sarah. Carlos was perched on Marmaduke's back, smiling at the camera.

Marmaduke laughed, but sounded nervous. "That's clearly the work of an amateur with horrendous graphic design skills."

He glanced around, but all the peds had skeptical looks on their faces—clearly, nobody believed him. Dogs started to shake their heads and leave the party.

"What a loser," a Pomeranian muttered.

A poodle sniffed loudly. "Liar."

"Wait, guys!" Marmaduke called. "It's not what you think! I'm still the same guy!"

A cocker spaniel paused at the front door. "I knew he was a phony."

Then everyone headed out as Marmaduke watched helplessly.

Bosco muscled up to Marmaduke smugly. "In the end," he said, "pedigrees always win. That's the way it will always be. Enjoy the rest of your party, mutt." Bosco nodded toward Jezebel, who was standing near Marmaduke, looking stricken. "Come on."

Jezebel didn't move. Her eyes shifted back and forth between Marmaduke and Bosco uncertainly before finally settling on Marmaduke. "Is it true?" she asked.

Marmaduke just stared at her silently, his eyes filled with shame.

"Jezebel!" Bosco barked. "Let's go!"

Shaking her head sadly, Jezebel followed Bosco outside.

His heart aching, Marmaduke looked around at the empty, trashed house, and his whole body drooped.

Carlos padded into the living room doorway, and Marmaduke turned to face him.

"What just happened?" Marmaduke asked.

"I think it's called a colossal fall from grace," Carlos replied. *"Hermano."*

Marmaduke stared out the window at the last of the peds disappearing down the block. Then his gaze settled on Mazie, Raisin, and Giuseppe looking back at him from the sidewalk across the street. He sighed with regret.

The mutts stared back at Marmaduke for a moment longer, and then they, too, headed off into the darkness.

"Not to rub salt in the wound," Carlos said, "but you kind of deserved it." Then Carlos spotted something on the carpet. "Hey, a cheese ball!" The cat pounced and munched on the snack.

Marmaduke sighed and curled up on the couch, more miserable than he'd ever been in his life.

He was still snoring on the couch when the Winslows arrived home in the morning.

Barbara opened the front door, carrying her luggage. "I can't wait for the next family boat trip," she said sarcastically.

"It was a weekend on a boat, okay?" Phil argued.

Debbie appeared in the doorway. "It wasn't a weekend, Phil—it was a workend. We spent two days watching you and Don work on your laptops."

"I know it wasn't ideal," Phil said, "but we had to get it done. Everything is riding on this presentation." He patted the laptop bag hanging from his shoulder, and then he turned and looked into the house.

Phil's mouth dropped open in shock when he saw the total disaster that was his home. "No, no, no," he babbled. "Marmaduke!"

Marmaduke sat up groggily on the couch. "I'm up!"

"Off the couch!" Phil hollered. "Now!"

As soon as Marmaduke's paws hit the floor, Phil scrambled after him. Marmaduke galloped into the kitchen and ran out the doggie door, but Phil stayed hot on his heels, yanking open the door to chase him across the lawn. Debbie and the kids were close behind.

"Bad dog!" Phil yelled. "Come here!"

"Phil, stop it!" Debbie shouted.

As Marmaduke reached the pool, Phil almost grabbed him, but missed.

Phil's laptop popped out of his shoulder bag and tumbled in the air.

It landed in the pool with a splash.

Phil stood at the edge of the pool, his hands on either side of his head. "The presentation," he moaned.

"Uh-oh," little Sarah said.

That night, a big storm lashed the town, rain pelting against the Winslows' windows. Phil and Debbie had worked all day cleaning up in silence, and they were just finishing straightening up the living room.

"I don't care if it is raining," Phil said through his gritted teeth, "I'm done. He's got a doghouse. He can sleep outside."

Debbie wiped dog spit off the wall. "Perfect," she said. "I'm sure that will solve everything. Maybe we can lock him on a chain in the backyard for the next ten years."

Phil straightened a set of scratched and torn

books. "Or maybe we could just give him away," he replied.

Marmaduke winced from where he was listening through the doggie door in the kitchen.

"You didn't just say that," Debbie said.

"It's an option we haven't explored yet," Phil countered. "That's all I'm saying."

Marmaduke turned around and walked sadly into the rain.

Phil and Debbie weren't done with their argument. "I don't understand you sometimes," Debbie said, sounding exasperated.

"He destroyed our home," Phil pointed out.

Debbie shook her head. "No, he didn't," she said. "Home is us. It's you, me, and the kids. It doesn't matter where we are."

Phil plopped down on the torn couch and crossed his arms. "It's just not how I imagined this move working out."

With a sigh, Debbie sat beside him. "The only way this move was going to work out was if we were in it together. But you seem to have totally lost sight of that."

Phil rubbed his hands over his face. "I worked my butt off this weekend, and yet again, the dog screwed it up."

"He's a dog, Phil," Debbie replied. "He doesn't know any better."

Phil just stared blankly at Debbie, until finally she stood up.

"You want him to sleep outside?" she asked. "Fine. He has a backyard . . . and you have a couch." She picked up a ripped pillow and a soiled blanket, and she tossed them to him.

Then she stormed upstairs, leaving Phil feeling chastened on the couch.

CHAPTER 9

Phil couldn't go to sleep—he still had the presentation to give tomorrow, so he worked on the family computer. The storm outside seemed to be getting worse all the time.

By the time Phil finished up, his eyes were red and sore, and he was exhausted. He flopped down on the couch.

Upstairs, Debbie tossed and turned, sleepless in bed.

Outside, Marmaduke lay under the eaves of the pool house, sleeplessly staring out at the rain.

Finally, Marmaduke gave up trying to nod off. He stood up and took one last look at the darkened house. Then he picked up Pig Cow, and walked out of the yard through the front gate.

Watching from the kitchen window, Carlos

was the only one who saw him leave.

Marmaduke carried Pig Cow through the rainy streets, getting splashed by passing cars as he walked miserably across the neighborhood.

He was completely soaked by the time he arrived at Mazie's house. Marmaduke stood in the driveway, dripping as he sadly stared at the garage door.

Marmaduke placed Pig Cow down carefully in front of the door. It let out a low *oink*. He sighed, and then turned and walked away.

"Who's there?" Mazie barked inside.

The garage door opened slowly. Mazie peered out under the door and then stepped outside when the door had risen high enough. She scanned the driveway and the street, but didn't see anyone.

Then she spotted Pig Cow lying nearby.

For a long moment, Mazie just stared at the squeaky toy. Her eyes welled up with sadness, and she lowered her head.

Pig Cow seemed to be staring back at her, reassuring her with its plastic smile. Mazie shook her head and took a deep breath, straightening herself up. "You know what?" she growled. "It's not that easy."

She grabbed Pig Cow with her mouth and strode briskly into the rain.

Walking at her fast pace, it wasn't too long before Mazie arrived at the Winslows'. She marched up to Marmaduke's doggie door and scratched on it.

After a few moments, Carlos peered out the doggie door.

Mazie spat Pig Cow out of her mouth. It landed on the back porch with a loud *oink*. "Tell the giant I'm not interested in a peace offering," she told Carlos.

"He's gone," Carlos replied. "He got busted with Phil and had to sleep outside tonight. He ran out the back gate about an hour ago."

A worried expression wrinkled up Mazie's muzzle. "Great," she sighed. "He has zero street smarts." She turned and headed out of the dark yard.

"Where are you going?" Carlos called after her.

"To find that big doofus!" Mazie shouted back.

Meanwhile, Marmaduke was wandering

around downtown. He rounded a corner in a shopping district, and a TV in an electronics store caught his attention. The TV showed a commercial with a family happily playing in their yard with their large dog. Marmaduke watched the commercial avidly until it switched to an ad for toothpaste. He shook his head sadly and kept walking. Marmaduke didn't have any destination in mind, but he didn't know what else to do.

As he crossed the street, a truck honked at him, and Marmaduke had to leap out of the way to avoid being run over. The truck ran through a big puddle, splashing Marmaduke with dirty water.

The rain, which had trickled out to a drizzle, picked up again when Mazie met up with Raisin outside the yacht club. "None of the strays in the pound have seen him," Mazie reported.

"He's not at the dog park, either," Raisin said, panting from running.

Giuseppe hurried over to the other mutts, wearing a waterlogged, puffy green sweater. "No luck," he gasped, also out of breath. He wriggled uncomfortably inside his sweater. "I knew

I shouldn't have worn wool. It's way too absorbent."

A streak of lightning flashed in the sky, and the three dogs glanced up at it. They shuddered at the clap of thunder that followed.

Giuseppe let out a nervous bark. "It's raining cats and us!" he complained.

"You guys head home," Mazie said. "I'm going to keep looking a little longer."

Raisin shook his head and snorted. "We can't leave you out here alone."

"It's too dangerous," Giuseppe added.

Then another clap of thunder echoed frighteningly all around them.

Both Giuseppe and Raisin's eyes were wide with fear. "See you later!" Raisin said.

"Yeah, good luck!" said Giuseppe.

They turned and ran off quickly, leaving Mazie alone in the storm.

Mazie headed inland, searching for Marmaduke in the tourist area near the waterfront. When she didn't see him there, she followed the railroad tracks toward the junkyard. "Marmaduke!" she called loudly. "Bark if you can hear me!"

When she received no reply, Mazie turned

the corner around the train station, determined to find him.

A few moments later, Marmaduke hurried over to the train station, looking for shelter. He'd just missed seeing Mazie. The station was completely closed up, so Marmaduke wandered back down the train tracks, hoping to find somewhere he could get out of the rain.

Then he spotted an opening in a copse of large bushes under a streetlamp. Marmaduke quickly ducked inside and was surprised to find himself in a cozy little hut built from the bushes' branches. There was even an old, ratty rug on the ground. He shook himself off, relieved to be out of the storm.

A noise inside the hut made Marmaduke's hackles rise—he wasn't alone in there! Marmaduke backed against a leafy wall, trying to identify the hulking, shadowy shape lurking in the rear of the hut.

The creature stepped forward into the light that streamed in from the streetlamp through the front opening of the hut.

Marmaduke gasped, feeling paralyzed with fear.

It was the dirty, scary-looking mastiff he'd seen on the way to the yacht club!

"Chupadogra," Marmaduke whispered, terrified.

The mastiff growled menacingly. "What are you doing in here?" he snarled.

"Please don't hurt me," Marmaduke begged.

With another growl, the mastiff paced closer to Marmaduke . . . but his growl turned into a rattling cough.

Marmaduke peered at the mastiff, who seemed older and frailer up close, although still frightening. "They say you went insane from rabies," Marmaduke whispered, "and that you sleep on a giant pile of your victim's bones. . . ."

The mastiff glared at Marmaduke for a long, tense moment, but then he shook his head and let out a hollow chuckle.

"Is it true?" Marmaduke asked.

"What do you care?" the mastiff replied. "You're going to think what you want anyway, right?"

Marmaduke wasn't sure if he should be scared anymore or not. "Uh," he said. "Sorry to bother you." He turned around to leave the bush hut.

"The railroad tracks are a pretty rough place at night," the mastiff called.

Marmaduke stopped and turned around, and then watched the mastiff step stiffly onto the old rug and creakily lie down on it. He and the mastiff stared at each other until Marmaduke got the feeling that the older dog was pretty lonely. He let out a long sigh.

"I don't even know what I'm doing anymore," Marmaduke admitted. "I acted like a big jerk and lost all my friends . . . and my family."

The mastiff nodded and rested his chin on his crossed paws. "All those stories, the nonsense about Chupadogra. Let me tell you, I used to be on top, I used to be King of the Hill." He coughed again softly. "But I turned my back on all my real friends and my family. And now I live out here alone, dodging trains and dogcatchers."

Marmaduke sat down on the edge of the rug. "I'm sorry," he said.

"I'm not looking for sympathy," the mastiff said sharply, raising his head, "and you shouldn't either. You did something stupid, and you got your nose rubbed in it. You're lucky. The ones who don't . . . they never learn."

"I feel like it's no use," Marmaduke said. "That no matter what I do, I'll always be the big freak who doesn't fit in."

The mastiff nodded, staring at Marmaduke with sympathy in his eyes. "I know what it's like to walk down the street and have everyone laugh and stare." He was a very big dog, too. "But what you need to understand is that you'll never truly fit in until you're comfortable in your own fur." He let out a whistling sigh. "I didn't learn that until it was too late. But you still have a chance. You have a home. Go there."

"What if I can't make things right?" Marmaduke asked.

The mastiff smiled. "There ain't no wrong too big to right."

Silently, Marmaduke thought about what the mastiff had said—it made a lot of sense. Then he noticed an old dog dish in the back of the hut. Faded letters on the side of the dish read BUSTER. "Thank you . . . Buster," he said.

"I stole that bowl from a dog I ate," the mastiff replied. "My name's Fred."

Marmaduke sat up straight and gulped nervously.

"Relax," the mastiff said with a laugh. "I'm pulling your collar."

With a sigh of relief, Marmaduke joined in with the mastiff's laughter.

That was when a truck roared up outside, headlights glaring into the hut, blinding them both.

"It's the dogcatchers!" the mastiff shouted. "Get out of here!"

But Marmaduke froze as the dogcatcher ran right at him. Just as he was about to grab Marmaduke, the mastiff jumped between them and growled at the man.

"Run!" the mastiff hollered. "Go home and make things right!"

"What about you?" Marmaduke barked back.

The mastiff flashed Marmaduke a devilish grin. "This ain't my first rodeo, kid." He snarled at the dogcatcher again, distracting him long enough so Marmaduke could scramble out of the hut into the rain.

"Let's make this easy, old timer," the dogcatcher told the mastiff.

"Just say the word, marshmallow," the mastiff growled back.

The bush hut shook with growls and yelps as the dogcatcher tried to catch the mastiff. Marmaduke didn't wait around to see what happened—he ran off into the stormy night.

In the morning, the rain had stopped and the wet lawn outside the Winslows' was glistening in the sunlight as the family gathered for breakfast. Without Marmaduke inside with them, the mood was subdued around the table.

Carlos scratched at Debbie's pants. "You've got to listen to me!" he meowed loudly. "Marmaduke is missing! He's been gone since last night!"

"You're a little talker this morning," Debbie cooed at him, patting him on the head. "Go eat your num-nums."

Sarah looked out the window. "Where's Marmaduke?" she asked worriedly.

Phil turned his head to look outside, too. The doghouse was empty, and there was no sign of the Great Dane anywhere. "Did he sneak back in with you?" he asked Debbie.

Debbie shook her head and then stood up to peer outside. "The back gate's open."

"That's what I've been saying!" Carlos yowled.

The family glanced around at one another, concerned looks on their faces.

"He'll be back, right?" asked Brian.

Barbara shivered. "He could get hit by a car . . ."

"If he's been gone all night," Debbie added, sounding upset, "anything could have happened."

Phil bit his lip. "I just wanted him to sleep outside, not run away." He glanced at his watch and frowned. "I've got the pitch to present this morning. If I don't nail it, I'm done."

"Just go," Debbie said curtly. "We'll find him."

Carlos peered up at Phil as he debated what he should do. "It's a no-brainer, Phil!" the cat screeched.

"No," Phil decided. "We'll all go find him." He grabbed his car keys off the counter, and the whole family got up from the table, snapping into action.

"Duh," Carlos meowed.

CHAPTER 10

Phil drove slowly through the downtown streets, craning his neck for any sign of Marmaduke. Debbie was peering through her window at the sidewalk on her side. Barbara was busy texting in the backseat, and Brian was on his cell phone. In her car seat between her siblings, Sarah couldn't see much, but she kept turning her head from side to side, hoping to catch a glimpse of her beloved pet.

"We can't find Marmaduke anywhere," Brian told a friend on the phone. "We really need your help. What do you mean, what does he look like? He's a Great Dane! He's like twice the size of your dog!"

Phil reached the end of town and paused at an intersection.

"Well, that's the neighborhood," Debbie said. "Where else could he be? The dog park?"

"He could be at the beach," Brian suggested.

"Guys, I'm texting everyone I know," said Barbara. "What if he's at the pound?"

"Good idea, Barb," Phil said. "Let's call them." He turned the car toward the beach as Debbie started dialing her phone to get the number for the pound.

Brian stuck his head out of the window. "Marmaduke!" he hollered. "Here, boy!"

A few minutes later, Phil cruised by the beach, but Marmaduke wasn't there. He steered back toward town so they could check out the dog park.

Meanwhile, Marmaduke had just reached the outskirts of downtown. He ran along a sidewalk, lost and talking to himself. "Come on," he muttered. "Give me something I can recognize . . . just one little landmark."

He headed toward a snarl of traffic a few streets away. As Marmaduke got closer, he could see police cars, fire trucks, and emergency road crews blocking an intersection. A giant water main had burst, creating a huge sinkhole in the middle of the street.

"Keep everyone out of here," an emergency technician told a police officer. "This sinkhole's growing fast! The whole road could collapse any minute!"

On the other side of the roadblock, Mazie hurried in front of a street of boutiques, sniffing everything she passed. "Come on, give me a scent," she said to herself. "One little, funky Marmaduke smell . . ."

Down the block, Phil was forced to stop the car when he reached the end of the traffic jam. "Oh, come on," he complained. "Not today."

The car's speaker phone rang, and Phil glanced at the caller ID. "It's Don." He pressed a button to connect the call. "Hi, Don."

"Winslow," Don asked angrily, "where the heck are you? You were supposed to be here an hour ago!"

Phil breathed through his teeth. "I'm sorry, Don," he said, "but we still haven't found Marmaduke yet. I just don't think I'm going to make it in today."

"I don't think you are either, because you're fired, Winslow!" Don shouted. He paused for a moment, and then in a calmer voice, he added, "I hope you find your dog." Then Don hung up.

Phil sighed.

Brian leaned forward. "You okay, Dad?"

"Yeah," Phil replied.

"You sure?" Brian asked.

Phil nodded. "Yeah."

Debbie peered worriedly at Phil, but she reached over and squeezed his hand reassuringly.

Closer to the disaster area, Mazie suddenly spotted Marmaduke on the other side of all the road crews and cars. "Marmaduke?" she said, barely believing her eyes. "Marmaduke!"

"Mazie?" Marmaduke said, hearing her voice. "Mazie!"

The dogs ran toward each other, slipping through the blockade into the roped-off area around the sinkhole.

Excitedly, Marmaduke jumped onto the hood of a car, wagging his tail.

In the Winslows' car, Brian suddenly pointed out the window. "There he is!" he shouted.

"Where?" Phil demanded.

Then he saw where Marmaduke was, and his blood ran cold.

Just as Mazie reached the car Marmaduke was standing on, a huge roar shook the street. The sinkhole collapsed, and the road under Mazie's paws caved in. Asphalt crumbled downward around her, and she could see into a storm drain deep in the hole below. Wild, frothing water was rushing through the exposed drain.

"Mazie, hang on!" Marmaduke howled.

Mazie leaped toward solid ground, but she just managed to grab on with her front paws. She hung precariously onto the edge of the sinkhole. "Marmaduke!" she screamed.

As Marmaduke rushed over to her, Mazie scrambled desperately, struggling to hold on. The edge crumbled, and Mazie plummeted down into the storm drain. She hit the churning water with a splash and was whisked away by the rushing rapids.

"Mazie!" Marmaduke cried.

Down the street, Phil burst out of the car and ran toward Marmaduke. He tried to duck under a streamer of yellow tape, but he was stopped by a firefighter.

"Stay back!" the firefighter shouted.

Phil feinted right, but then ran left, jumping

past the firefighter. He kept hustling toward his dog. "Marmaduke!" he yelled.

Marmaduke didn't hear him. He stared down into the sinkhole, barking. Then the Great Dane took a deep breath and leaped into the rushing water.

Phil stopped short, shocked by Marmaduke's action. He whirled around and faced the firefighter who had chased him. "Where does this open up?" he demanded to know.

"Catch basin," the firefighter replied. "Two blocks down." He raised his walkie-talkie to his face. "We got two dogs in the water," he reported. "Repeat: two dogs in the water."

Phil took off running down the street with the firefighter following close behind.

They zoomed past two skaters gawking nearby. One of them pulled out a phone and started recording a video as the skaters trailed after Phil and the firefighter.

Inside the storm drain, Mazie struggled desperately to stay afloat as the rough water washed her along at breakneck speed. Marmaduke dog-paddled forcefully after her, getting closer.

"I'm coming, Mazie!" he howled.

Up above, Phil caught a ride on a fire truck that was heading toward the catch basin. With the truck's siren blaring, they arrived at a large manhole quickly.

Phil hopped out of the fire truck, along with a group of firefighters. One carried a winch. They rushed toward the manhole, and the firefighters pulled out tools to open it.

In the cold water, Mazie was losing her battle with exhaustion. She paddled frantically, but it was no use—she started to slip under the water.

Before she sunk, Marmaduke surged forward and snagged her collar with his teeth. He held her head above the waterline as they were washed down the pipe together.

Up ahead of them in the tunnel, a bright beam of sunlight appeared as the manhole opened up in the ceiling. The firefighters slid the winch into place and immediately lowered a firefighter on a tether into the water.

The firefighter grabbed Mazie as she slammed into him. He slipped her into a sling. "Got one!" the firefighter announced into his walkie-talkie.

Then the firefighter turned to Marmaduke, who was swimming against the current a few feet away. "Come on, boy!" he shouted, gesturing for Marmaduke to swim closer.

Before Marmaduke could move, a terrifying roar filled the tunnel. He glanced back the way he'd come and saw a huge surge of water hurtling toward him.

Up on the street, Phil peered down into the manhole, trying to see what was going on below. He was surrounded by firefighters hard at work trying to rescue the dogs. "Anything?" Phil asked.

One firefighter raised his walkie-talkie. "What's your status?"

A cold wave of fear rushed over Phil as he heard the roar of the surge below. The winch sagged, and static issued from the walkie-talkie.

Everyone looked down the manhole, but it was too dark down there to make out what was going on.

Phil's pulse pounded in his ears.

After a long, stressful moment, Mazie's face appeared over the edge of the manhole, and then the firefighter below pushed her all the way out. An EMT grabbed her and whisked her away from the manhole.

"Marmaduke!" Mazie howled.

The tethered firefighter was hoisted up. He sat on the edge of the manhole, coughing up water.

"Where's the other one?" Phil asked. "Where's Marmaduke?"

The wet firefighter shook his head. "Sorry," he coughed. "He was too big. I . . . lost him."

Phil looked around at the other firefighters, who all stared back at him somberly. He had never felt so helpless in his life.

Then Phil tightened his hands to fists. "No," he said firmly. "No, you don't understand. We can't give up." He gestured down at the pipe. "Where does this go?"

The sitting firefighter pointed across a nearby bridge. "The aqueduct," he replied.

Phil didn't hesitate—he took off running.

On the small footbridge over the flooded concrete canyon of the aqueduct, Phil paused to peer over the edge. He spotted a giant shadow in the rapids below.

Without a second thought, Phil climbed up on the bridge railing.

"Get off there!" a firefighter shouted. "It's too dangerous!"

Phil jumped.

He landed in the cold water with a big splash and immediately started swimming toward the underwater shadow he'd seen. When Phil reached it, he stuck his hand deep into the water and grabbed onto Marmaduke by the back of his neck.

With a mighty yank, Phil pulled Marmaduke's head out of the water.

Marmaduke gasped for air.

Phil clutched onto the big dog as the water smashed them into a huge fallen tree that had jammed against the aqueduct wall. He pushed Marmaduke onto a branch, and Phil caught hold of another branch a little way downstream.

"Marmaduke!" Phil shouted. "Come!"

His sides heaving, Marmaduke seemed drained as the rapids continued to pummel him.

Phil got his arm around the tree trunk, and he pulled himself up onto it. He struggled to climb to his feet.

A firefighter threw a safety line over the side of the aqueduct, and Phil grabbed it and quickly wrapped it around himself.

"Marmaduke!" Phil yelled. "I can't get to you!

You have to come!"

Marmaduke shook his head—he was too scared to move.

"Marmaduke, I need you to come!" Phil hollered.

"I can't!" Marmaduke barked back. "I'm too big!" He looked over at Phil, his eyes wild with panic.

Phil stared directly into the Great Dane's eyes. "I won't let you go, Marmaduke," Phil said calmly and confidently. "I promise. Come."

With a deep breath, Marmaduke mustered up his courage. He let go of the branch and flopped his big body toward Phil.

Phil grabbed him. With all his might, he heaved Marmaduke up onto the tree trunk with him. "You're safe now, buddy," he whispered.

"Harness coming down!" a firefighter hollered over the side of the footbridge.

Glancing up, Phil saw a large harness on a rope dropping down beside him. He quickly wrapped the harness around Marmaduke's chest.

The rope grew taut as the firefighter heaved on it, and Marmaduke swung in the air toward the bridge.

Marmaduke's eyes rolled as he lurched upward. "I still hate water!" he moaned.

Ten minutes later, Phil and Marmaduke were safe on dry land. They sat together in the back of a parked ambulance, both of them wrapped in blankets. Nearby, Mazie was being toweled off by a firefighter. Everyone looked exhausted but thrilled to be alive.

"I know you won't understand any of this," Phil told Marmaduke, "but I've never been so happy to see your giant, drooling face. And I'm done trying to be some fake Top Dog. A real Top Dog watches out for his family." He hugged Marmaduke. "And you are family."

That's it, I can't stand it anymore, Marmaduke thought. *I'm gonna kiss him.* He wrapped his paws around Phil's neck and slobbered on his face.

Phil laughed and hugged Marmaduke tighter, and then started scratching his lower back.

That's the spot! Marmaduke thought, writhing in happiness. *Oh, that's so nice . . . I've got to bite the air. . . .*

Marmaduke managed to chomp at the air only a few times before Debbie, Barbara, Brian, and Sarah rushed over and hugged him and Phil. They laughed and cried at the same time, so happy to be together.

Phil put his arm around Marmaduke and smiled at his family. "I love you guys so much," he said softly, "and I want you to know, I realize this has all been my fault. I guess I tried to turn us all into something we're not by moving out here. I'm really sorry."

The kids smiled at their father.

"What I'm trying to say is," Phil continued, "I think we should move back to Kansas."

"Kansas?" Marmaduke barked.

"What?" cried Barbara.

"That's crazy talk, Dad," Brian said.

Phil shook his head in confusion. "But I thought you guys weren't happy here—"

He was interrupted by a bunch of skaters running up to them. One was waving a cell phone. "Dude," one skater gushed, "that was awesome! We got it all on camera! We're putting it up on the internet!"

"Thanks, I guess," Phil replied. He glanced back at his family. "So . . . you guys want to stay here?"

Debbie nodded and put her arm around her children. "Honey, we fit here," she explained. "We fit in our house, we fit . . . well, we don't fit in the company car, but—"

Phil smiled and kissed her.

"We just missed you," Debbie finished.

Once again, Phil pulled his family close for a hug. "Well, if we're all together on this, then guess what, Winslows! We're home."

A dalmatian from one of the fire trucks was sitting nearby and had overheard everything. A tear rolled down his muzzle, and he wiped it away with his paw. "I've been on this crew nine years," the dalmatian sobbed, "and that's some pretty strong stuff."

CHAPTER 11

A few days later, Phil took Marmaduke to the dog park. He unleashed him when they arrived at the meadow. "Go play, buddy," Phil urged.

Marmaduke ran off, his ears flapping. As he loped across the lawn, he looked at the other side of the meadow and saw Bosco sitting back in his spot in the shade of the palm trees. He was surrounded by Jezebel, Thunder, Lightning, and many other peds.

Here goes nothing, Marmaduke thought. He took a deep breath and slowly let it out. Then he started running toward the pedigrees.

On his way, Marmaduke passed Raisin and Giuseppe, who were lying in the shade under a patchy rosebush.

"Hey, check it out," Raisin said.

Giuseppe peered at Marmaduke. "What the heck's he doing?"

Most of the dogs in the park noticed where Marmaduke was headed, and they all paid close attention. Some of them even whispered, "Fight, fight," to one another.

Marmaduke slowed down as he got closer to the palms, but he still strode purposefully until he reached Bosco.

"What's up, big boy?" Bosco asked lazily. "You here to exact revenge?"

"Actually, no, Bosco," Marmaduke replied. "I'm going to thank you."

Bosco chuckled. "Thank me for what?"

"For showing me how stupid I was," answered Marmaduke calmly. "I don't care what everyone thinks of me, because it doesn't matter if you're big or small, or a pedigree or a mutt. We're all just dogs. That's the way the park should be." He smiled, showing all his teeth. "So I'm going to sit down and claim this spot for all the dogs who don't think they have what it takes to be over here."

With that speech, Marmaduke sat down in front of Bosco and stared at him.

"Are you kidding me?" Bosco asked, hopping to his feet. He moved up into Marmaduke's face and growled.

Marmaduke didn't budge.

Then, one by one, other dogs in the park came over and sat down next to Marmaduke. The dogs were all sizes, all shapes, all colors, and all breeds or mixes of breeds. They all stared at Bosco.

Bosco couldn't believe his eyes. "Does everyone have rabies-induced insanity?" he demanded. "This is pedigree turf!"

More dogs arrived to join Marmaduke, until he was surrounded by dozens of supporters. Quickly Bosco became totally outnumbered.

"You're all just mutts!" Bosco howled. "All of you!" He nodded his head toward Jezebel. "Let's go, Jezebel," he said.

Jezebel sat down. "I kind of like sitting here, too."

Bosco gaped at her in disbelief.

"Me too," Thunder said. He sat next to Jezebel.

His eyes wide, Bosco looked pleadingly at Lightning.

"I always thought I was too short," Lightning

said, "but I'm done taking your crap, dude. It's my park, too." He sat down on the other side of Jezebel and then turned to call out to Raisin and Giuseppe. "Come have a seat, fellas!"

Raisin and Giuseppe trotted over and took a seat.

"Feel the breeze," Raisin said blissfully.

Giuseppe relaxed for maybe the first time in his life. "I can see forever."

"Have it your way, losers," Bosco snarled. "I'll remember this. Payback is going to hurt."

Right then, a bee buzzed down and landed on Bosco's nose. Bosco's eyes crossed as he stared at it in alarm.

"Bee!" he shrieked, and he scampered away from the palms.

The dogs sitting beside Marmaduke all let out happy howls of victory.

Jezebel leaned gently against Marmaduke. "Ever think you'd do something like that?"

"Of course," Marmaduke replied. "I used to be alpha dog, remember?" He smiled at her, but then ducked his head a little nervously. "Listen," he said, "I don't know how to say this without hurting your feelings—"

Jezebel silenced him by covering his mouth with her paw. "Shh," she said. "I'll be fine. It's time to stand on my own four legs a while. Besides, we'll still be friends."

"Ouch," Marmaduke said. "I hate it when girls say that."

They smiled at each other, but Marmaduke looked away when he noticed that all the dogs were staring at something coming across the lawn.

Marmaduke was stunned by what he saw.

It was Mazie. She sauntered across the grass confidently. Her coat was clean and gleaming, freshly groomed to remove all the tangles. She looked gorgeous, with a small pink bow in her hair.

"Hello, doggie!" Thunder panted.

Lightning wiggled his whole body. "Va-va-voom!"

With a nervous gulp, Marmaduke stood up and strode over to Mazie. "You look amazing," he told her.

"I feel like a fluffy monstrosity," Mazie replied.

"Look," Marmaduke said, lowering his voice. "I wanted to say sorry for how I've been acting. I was a real jerk, and you didn't deserve it. I think my brain turned into a cocker spaniel's for a while." He leaned over to whisper to a nearby cocker spaniel, "No offense."

The cocker spaniel blinked blankly at Marmaduke. "Huh?"

Mazie tilted her head, thinking over Marmaduke's words. She smiled. "It takes a big dog to admit that."

Marmaduke returned her grin. "You want to walk over to the fire hydrant and catch up?" he asked. "I'll fill you in on how I just abolished class warfare in the park."

As they headed toward the fire hydrant together, Mazie bumped gently into Marmaduke. "You're kind of my hero, by the way," she admitted. "But don't let it go to your head. I hear you're prone to doing that."

"Burn," replied Marmaduke.

They sauntered past Phil, who was walking toward Don.

Don spotted Phil and hurried toward him. "Winslow!" he called. "I've been looking for you everywhere!"

Phil shook his head. "But I thought you fired me."

"Oh, don't be so sensitive," Don said, shrugging. "Any man that chooses his dog over his career is an idiot . . . and that's just the kind of idiot I want working for me! Besides, have you seen the number of hits your rescue of Marmaduke has gotten on the internet? Six hundred eighty-two thousand and climbing! We're going to sell a lot of dog food!"

"Wow!" Phil exclaimed. "That's . . . unbelievable!"

Don waved his hand for Phil to follow him as he started to walk barefoot on the grass. "Come on," he said. "We've got a lot of work to do."

Out in the meadow, all the dogs howled their approval as Marmaduke and Mazie shared a long, lingering kiss.

Watching on a bench from afar was Carlos. "From Kansas zero to O.C. hero," the cat said warmly. "It makes me proud."

Then a female cat who looked almost exactly like Carlos jumped up onto the bench next to him.

"Hi, there," the female cat purred. "Is this spot taken?"

Carlos waggled his eyebrows. "It is now," he replied. "Tell me, do you believe in *amor* at first sight?"